"Tell me you felt nothing," Tyler said. "Tell me you felt nothing, and I'll leave."

Tyler watched her, his breath stopping in his chest. He suddenly realized that he couldn't breathe until he heard her response. What if she told him that she'd felt nothing?

But she didn't. Instead, she sighed in frustration and turned back to the door.

Vindicated, Tyler placed a hand on her shoulder and turned her. Then he placed a finger under her chin and forced her to look at him.

Slowly, Nya met his gaze, her eyes glistening beneath the house lights. Damn, she looked so darn kissable.

So irresistible.

Tyler slipped his hand around her waist and pulled her against him. A soft sigh escaped her as her body landed against his. The feel of those breasts against his chest… He wanted her.

"Seems you need me to kiss you again in order for you to give me an answer." He paused, ran the pad of his thumb over her bottom lip. "So I'm going to do that. And then I want an answer."

Dear Reader,

It's been so much fun writing about sexy firefighters that I have to wonder why I haven't done this before! I know how much you love connecting stories, so you'll be happy that Nya and Tyler get their love story here.

Perhaps this scenario sounds familiar. You've searched high and low for love, and been disappointed time and time again. So now you've given up. You've been hurt too many times to believe that the possibility of love really exists for you.

That's where Nya is. After one too many hopeless dates, she's decided to take a hiatus from dating altogether. But you know what they say about the best laid plans. Suddenly Tyler comes into her life, throwing her dating hiatus into a tailspin. What do you do when your brain and heart aren't on the same page…and the chemistry is off the charts?

I hope you enjoy the heat between Nya and Tyler!

Kayla

Flames
OF
PASSION

Kayla Perrin

⟨H⟩ **HARLEQUIN**® KIMANI™ ROMANCE

Recycling programs
for this product may
not exist in your area.

ISBN-13: 978-0-373-86385-3

Flames of Passion

For questions and comments about the quality of this book please contact us at CustomerService@Harlequin.com.

Printed in U.S.A.

TM www.Harlequin.com

Kayla Perrin has been writing since the age of thirteen and once entertained the idea of becoming a teacher. Instead, she has become a *USA TODAY* and *Essence* bestselling author of dozens of mainstream and romance novels and has been recognized for her talent, including twice winning Romance Writers of America's Top Ten Favorite Books of the Year Award. She has also won the Career Achievement Award for multicultural romance from *RT Book Reviews*. Kayla lives with her daughter in Ontario, Canada. Visit her at kaylaperrin.com.

Books by Kayla Perrin

Harlequin Kimani Romance

Island Fantasy
Freefall to Desire
Taste of Desire
Always in My Heart
Surrender My Heart
Heart to Heart
Until Now
Burning Desire
Flames of Passion

Visit the Author Profile page at
Harlequin.com for more titles

For Sharon,

You've been waiting patiently for your
Mr. Right. But don't worry. You know what they say…
When you least expect it, he'll appear.
And he will definitely be worth the wait!

Chapter 1

Nya Lowe gazed across the lavish hotel reception hall and nearly choked on the shrimp appetizer she had just plopped into her mouth. Her heart began to beat rapidly, and a chill slid down her spine.

Oh, God, tell me that is not *Russell!*

As she watched that familiar swagger and saw that overly cheerful smile, Nya's stomach sank.

Russell Ewing.

Russell Ewing, the man who had taken her to a restaurant to publicly dump her, when she'd been fool enough to believe he was going to propose.

The man she couldn't get over, no matter how many bad dates she went on.

Turning abruptly, Nya hurried the few steps over to the bar, where she squeezed herself between the wall of men gathered there. Hopefully, Russell hadn't seen her.

"What can I get you?" the bartender asked her almost immediately.

"Um…" Nya reached into her purse. "I've got this drink ticket." Each attendee at the gala to celebrate the launch of the Ocean City Firefighters' Calendar had received two drink tickets. "Can it get me a White Zinfandel?"

"Of course."

As Nya watched the bartender pour her drink, she became aware of the fact that her breathing was all but nonexistent. It was as though Russell had sucked all the air out of the room.

She glanced over her shoulder and felt a spurt of panic. Russell was heading in her direction.

Even worse, there was a stunning, curvaceous woman on his arm. A woman Nya recognized. Topaz Gem—clearly a pseudonym—was the lead actress whom Russell had cast in his independent film.

Were they a couple?

"There you go," the bartender said, and Nya was grateful that she needed to turn her attention back to him.

Nya was tempted to down the wine and promptly purchase another one. Then she asked herself, *Why are you letting Russell get to you?*

It was likely that she could go the whole evening without even running into him. There were enough attendees at the gala that two people could never even cross paths.

She glanced over her shoulder again. And her heart just about imploded. Not only was Russell heading in her direction, his eyes connected with hers.

He smiled.

Nya took a liberal sip of her drink as her brain scrambled to figure out what to do. Should she simply walk away?

Walk? Heck, she wanted to run as fast and far as her four-inch heels would take her.

But running would make her look like a coward. Or worse, it would make her look like she was still hung up on Russell.

Russell waved, making it clear that she'd lost her chance to flee. There went her plan of pretending that she hadn't seen him.

Nya swallowed. Darn it, she wasn't prepared to talk to him. She wasn't prepared to make nice with Topaz Gem, either, who was clinging to him as if he were Denzel Washington. She had never liked Topaz, who had overtly flirted with Russell after she was cast in the film. Nya had feared that Russell had crossed the line with her but had never had any proof. Now, however, she had to wonder if Topaz had been the reason behind their breakup…

Oh, God. He's getting closer! What was she going to do?

No particular plan in mind, Nya found herself trailing her fingers down the arm of the man beside her. Stunned, his gaze whipped to hers.

Nya looped her arm through his. "Just go with it," she whispered.

The man, whom she now recognized as one of the firefighters featured in the calendar, narrowed his eyes in confusion.

"Baby," Nya purred moments before Russell reached her. "It's not polite to ignore me for so long."

"I'm sorry?"

"It's okay, I forgive you." And before he could say another word, Nya eased up on her toes, snaked a hand around his neck and pulled his head down. And then she kissed him.

She kissed him brazenly, despite the fact that they were in public. Her tongue forced his lips open, then slipped into his mouth. As she made out with this stranger, Nya was aware of just how delectable his lips were. Not to mention how amazing his muscular body felt pressed against hers.

Kissing him with the kind of passion reserved for the bedroom, Nya strummed her fingers along his neck. She could feel the man's surprise in the way his athletic body had tensed, but soon, he gave in and kissed her back.

Breaking free of him with an exaggerated moan of desire, Nya eased back. She shot a glance to her right, and yes! Russell was standing right there, staring at her with an unguarded look of surprise.

"Oh, hi," Nya said breathlessly. She placed her hand on the firefighter's chest, whom she now recognized to be Tyler Something-Or-Other. When he'd come into the studio where Nya worked to be photographed, she'd thought he was especially attractive.

Everyone was there tonight to celebrate the launch of the calendar, which Sabrina, her best friend and exceptional photographer, had created. The Ocean City Fire Department had been thrilled with Sabrina's final product, and the fund-raising gala they'd thrown had been going remarkably well.

Until Nya had seen Russell.

"Good evening, Nya," Russell said. His eyes flitted from Nya to Tyler.

"Wow," Nya said, her tone bright, "it's been a long time."

"A year and a half," Russell said.

"Since we broke up," Nya said. "But it's been a year and two months since we last saw each other. Not that I'm counting."

"Something like that."

Nya did her best not to glare at him. Instead, she concentrated on trying to prove to him that she had moved on. "Russell, I want you to meet Tyler. My boyfriend." The smile on her face was so fake that it hurt, but she'd be damned if she would let Russell feel any sense of power over her. He may have broken her heart, but he was going to see that she was over him.

Russell extended his hand to Tyler. "Tyler. Good to meet you. I'm Russell Ewing."

"Tyler McKenzie," Tyler said, pumping Russell's hand. "Firefighter."

"Yep, he's a firefighter," Nya gushed.

"Ah," Russell said. "A firefighter. One of our city's first responders. I salute you."

Topaz's eyebrows shot up. "Yes! You're November. I saw your picture. Very sexy."

"That's me," Tyler said.

"I didn't quite recognize you out of your uniform," Topaz went on.

Nya's eyes widened with alarm at the way Topaz's eyelashes fluttered. Was she flirting with her pretend man?

Nya held on to Tyler a little more proprietarily. Topaz had already stolen one man of hers, and she wasn't about to let her sink her teeth into her new fake boyfriend, as well.

Russell also didn't look happy.

"You remember Topaz," Russell said, snaking his arm around her waist.

"Topaz," Nya said, without an ounce of enthusiasm. "Good to see you again."

"Likewise," Topaz replied, barely able to force a smile on her face as she spoke. The tension only made it more apparent to Nya that Topaz *had* been involved with Russell while they'd been dating.

Nya wanted to ask her how long she had been sleeping with her boyfriend, and if it had started the moment Russell had cast her for his film. But she didn't bother. She was over Russell. All she wanted now was for him to know it.

"Russell and I are dating!" Topaz announced. "A little over a year and a half now."

"More like a year and a few months," Russell said, then chuckled uneasily.

Year and a half! Russell had *definitely* been cheating on her!

"Oh, right," Topaz said, catching on. "A year and a few months. We were working together and couldn't deny our attraction."

Not wanting to hear another word, Nya turned to the bar and began to search in her purse for her second drink ticket. She needed another alcoholic beverage, and fast.

Nya ordered a vodka tonic and promptly took a liberal sip.

When she turned around and tuned in to the conversation again, Russell was asking, "So how long have you two been together?"

"Not too—" Tyler began.

"Six months," Nya interjected. "Six *amazing* months." Six months ago was the last time Nya had contacted Russell, foolishly asking if they could once again work on their relationship. He hadn't told her that he'd been involved with Topaz, but he had told her that she needed to move on.

"Great," Russell said. "I'm glad you're happy."

"We're *very* happy," Nya said, and placed a hand on Tyler's chest.

Feeling a jolt of heat, she withdrew her hand. And took another sip of her drink.

"Listen," Russell began, "I'm glad I ran into you. I finally finished the film. And the premiere is this Friday night. I would love for you and Tyler to come."

"You finished it?" Nya asked. "Wow." It was bittersweet. She had been working with Russell on the film, wearing many hats as he'd been trying to produce his first feature. Their breakup had meant the end of her involvement on the project, one she'd believed in.

"Yep," Russell said. "And it's time to introduce my baby to the world."

At Russell's statement, Topaz leaned into him, and Nya wanted to roll her eyes. *He's not referring to you, dimwit.*

Instead, Nya also moved closer to Tyler, taking his hand in hers. "I'm really happy for you, Russell," she said in a sweet tone. "But I'm sorry. I'm busy Friday night. Tyler and I have plans."

Tyler, who up until this point had been mostly silent, suddenly spoke. "Actually, that dinner fell through."

Nya's eyes shot to his. "Honey?"

"We can make it to Russell's screening." Then he faced Russell. "What time will it be?"

Nya wanted to elbow him in the ribs. What was he doing? Yes, she had kissed him without warning, but surely he must have figured out that she was playing a role. All she wanted him to do was look hot and stay silent.

"Seven o'clock," Russell said. "And there'll be an after party, as well. At The Diamond Club."

"Ooh, one of the best hot spots." Tyler leaned in close and kissed Nya on the temple. "We'll be there."

Russell beamed. "Excellent! It's a great film, if I do say so myself."

"What's the film about?" Tyler asked.

"Struggling alcoholic with an abusive past finds herself and redemption," Russell answered.

Nya cleared her throat. "Sweetie," she began, an undeniable edge to her tone. "Are you sure Friday night's engagement dinner is canceled? Because when I spoke to Jennifer, she said she was only waiting on confirmation from her brother." Turning to Russell, Nya explained. "Jen's brother is on the East Coast, and he's working on a huge ad campaign and isn't sure he'll be able to leave town. But he'll know by tomorrow. Which is why we can't confirm with Russell," Nya went on, looking at Tyler now. "Knowing Keith, he'll be on a flight early Friday morning to make sure he gets here. I'm sure it will go ahead, as planned."

Tyler was shaking his head even before she was finished with her story. "Nope," he said. "I spoke with Dave. He told me it's definitely canceled. Keith didn't want to be rushed, so they decided to put off the dinner. Jen doesn't want to have the dinner without him being there. After all, he's the only family she's got left."

Nya could smack Tyler. Truly, she could. Why was he throwing a wrench into her well-executed excuse? Wasn't it apparent to him that she was trying to *avoid* Russell? Weren't firefighters supposed to *save* people? Didn't he see that she needed saving?

For some crazy reason, Tyler seemed determined to beat her at her own game.

He winked at her. Then he looked at Russell. "We'd love to come."

Resignation swirling in Nya's gut like black tar, she faced Russell. "All right, then. Since the dinner is canceled, we'll be there."

Russell clapped his hands together. "Excellent." Then he reached into his jacket pocket and produced two tickets. "Here you go. These will get you into the premiere."

Tyler took them. "Thank you."

"I'm the lead actress," Topaz said to Tyler. "It's my first big role."

"Great," Tyler said. "I look forward to it."

With a nod, Russell said, "We'd better continue making the rounds. More people to see."

"Don't let us stop you," Nya said, her fake smile still plastered on her face.

"Good to see you again, Nya." Then, finally, Russell turned and walked away. Topaz turned, casting a lingering glance at Tyler as she started walking off with Russell.

The nerve!

The moment they were out of earshot, Nya turned to Tyler. "What did you think you were doing?"

"Tyler McKenzie," Tyler said, offering her his hand. "Pleasure to make your acquaintance."

Nya glared at him. "I know who you are. I work at the photography studio with Sabrina."

"Ahhh, that's right." He snapped a finger. "That's why you looked familiar."

"Nya," she told him, a little hurt that he didn't remember her. "Nya Lowe."

"Now that we've been properly re-introduced, are you going to kiss me again?" Tyler asked.

Her face flaming, Nya forced in an even breath. Then she felt a measure of disgust. "You men. You're all the same."

Tyler chuckled. "Excuse me? You kiss me, then you look at me like *I'm* some sort of creep?"

"Don't you have a fiancée?" Nya asked. She remembered that he had mentioned his fiancée during the photo shoot and had dashed her hopes of dating him in the process.

"I did," Tyler said. "It ended about four months ago."

"Oh," Nya said, feeling stupid. "I see. I—I'm sorry."

"No, don't be sorry."

"That was my ex-boyfriend, and I needed someone," Nya explained.

"Happy to help."

Tyler grinned at her, a smile that was both charming and disarming. But still Nya wasn't impressed with his antics. "Obviously, you had to have realized that I was trying to *escape* Russell. Yet you accepted an invitation to a film I clearly don't want to go to. You're a firefighter. Don't firefighters rescue people?"

Tyler chuckled. "I've never quite had to *rescue* anyone in exactly that manner before..."

"You know what I mean," Nya said.

"You laid one on me without any explanation. If you wanted help, shouldn't you have just asked instead of kissing me?"

"You're right," Nya conceded. "Obviously, you had no clue what I was doing, and I'm sorry for the way I handled things. It's just, suddenly he was there, and I panicked." Nya paused, realizing that she was doing too much talking. "The problem is, you created a bigger mess for me by telling Russell that we'll go to the screening of his film."

"Or, what I've actually done is give you another opportunity to drive your point home."

"How so?"

"You clearly want to prove to this guy that you're over him. So why don't we get dressed up on Friday night and go to the movie premiere? After that, there'll be no doubt in his mind that you've moved on."

Nya's stomach fluttered. Just what was Tyler proposing to leave no doubt in Russell's mind? A night of hot kisses and close embraces?

"As much as I appreciate your willingness to help out," Nya said, "I'm going to refuse."

"Oh." Tyler's eyebrows rose, and a confused expression passed over his face.

"What?" Nya asked. "What's with that look?"

"It's just…I thought you kissed me because of your ex, but maybe that's not why at all."

"Excuse me?"

"I thought you used me to get to your ex, but maybe you were actually using your ex to get to me."

Chapter 2

Tyler didn't know why he was toying with Nya. But then, no strange woman had ever just kissed him out of the blue. Tyler was a hot-blooded male. When a woman as sexy as this one kissed you, you wanted more.

But given the look on her face right now, it was clear that the last thing on her mind was kissing him again. Those beautiful lips had parted, and indignation was flashing on her face.

"Excuse me?"

Tyler knew he should retract his statement, but even her anger was incredibly sexy.

"Maybe kissing me had nothing to do with your ex."

"You must be out of your mind." Nya's eyes blazed. "Of course I wasn't coming up with an excuse to kiss you. I was desperate, and you were there."

"Ouch," Tyler said. Her words stung more than he expected.

"Sorry," Nya said immediately. Closing her eyes, she exhaled sharply. "I didn't mean to sound so callous."

"I'm not sure I've ever been kissed—then insulted," Tyler said, still trying to keep the mood light. He wanted her at ease, because he still wanted her around.

"I didn't mean that." Nya groaned. "I'm sure women enjoy kissing you. Just not me."

"Double ouch."

"Can we please stop talking about this? I keep saying the wrong thing." Her chest rose and fell with another sigh, something that made Tyler's groin tighten. Nya was wearing a black formfitting dress with a low scoop neck that revealed the beautiful mounds of her breasts. Did she have any clue how delectable she looked?

"It's just," she went on, sounding frazzled, "seeing Russell tonight has thrown me for a loop. I really don't want to talk about him anymore."

Tyler had no interest in talking about Russell, either, but he wasn't ready to be done with Nya. She was stunning, and her kiss had stirred a desire in his gut that had long since been repressed. Oh, he definitely wasn't ready to be done with her. He wanted to take her out on Friday night, make her forget this Russell character for good.

"I don't want to talk about the guy, either," Tyler said. "But don't you want to quash his effect on you once and for all?"

"I don't know what you're talking about."

"It's clear he still gets to you."

"Not because I'm hung up on him."

"The problem is," Tyler went on, "if you don't go to the premiere on Friday night, he'll know he still has power over you The power to make you upset, or afraid…or to simply get under your skin. Why don't you flip the script on him?"

"Flip the script?" Nya asked.

"Yeah."

As Nya looked up into Tyler's dark eyes, she wasn't altogether concentrating on what he was saying. She was distracted by the fact that he was the definition of *smoking hot.* A firefighter being smoking hot…how appropriate was that?

"Russell is completely full of himself," Nya said. "He'll always feel he has power over me."

"Especially if you avoid the event on Friday night."

Tyler turned to the bar and took a pull of his beer. His blazer jacket slid back as he moved, giving Nya a glimpse of his physique beneath his white dress shirt. Damn, the man was fine. Even with clothes on, she could see that his body was well sculpted.

There was no doubt that he was exactly her type. And kissing him…she'd felt her body warm in all the right places.

Which was exactly why she couldn't go out with him on Friday night. After her last disastrous date, Nya had finally decided to go on a dating hiatus. Indefinitely. She'd examined her behavior and realized that she'd been going about trying to find love with a sense of desperation. Which of course had led to disaster.

The problem was, Nya didn't really know any other way to go about dating than to jump headfirst into a relationship. So she'd sworn off dating and was now trying to get to a place where she could accept being happy on her own.

Nya had analyzed why every relationship she'd had since Russell—and including her relationship with Russell, for that matter—had ended badly. And the glaring reason why things didn't work out was because Nya went for looks first, character later. If a man looked good and sounded smooth, Nya fell for him like a fool.

And Tyler had the kind of looks that could have her brain cells going on strike. So Nya didn't even want to put herself in the path of temptation.

She tried another tactic. "Obviously, you're a very attractive man. And you were gracious enough to…to kiss me back…and go along with my ruse. But a man as attractive as you must have several women vying for your attention. I don't expect you to give up a Friday night for me when you can spend it with someone you want to. I'll come up with a reason why we can't go to the film. You know what, it doesn't even matter if I have a reason or not. It's not like I have to answer to Russell."

"Then it's going to look like you're chickening out," Tyler said matter-of-factly. "Russell's going to know you made up an excuse not to see him again, and he'll see right through it. He'll think you're still hung up on him."

Nya felt a spasm of fear. She wished Tyler would stop saying that, because it was the one thing that was weakening her resolve.

"I can see that the truth is getting to you," Tyler went on. "And trust me, that's how guys think. You went to the trouble of kissing me to make a point to him. Seems as though it would be rather foolish to abandon the plan now when we can drive the point home on Friday night."

Nya bit her inner cheek as she thought. She hated to admit it, but Tyler had a point. Russell was that kind of guy. Even when he'd dumped her, he'd rubbed salt in her wound by saying that she would never find another decent guy because she was too clingy.

He had been right about her not being able to find another man, but the part about her being clingy? Nya wasn't clingy, and he had hurt her deeply when he'd said that.

And still, she had foolishly reached out to him during a time when she had been weak and needed a sexual fix. She had remembered only the good times between them and forgotten the hurt. It was her selective memory that had led her to call Russell nine months earlier when she had been lonely. She'd invited him over, telling him that there would be no strings attached, that she just wanted him for one night. He'd come over, and they'd made love. But in the morning, Russell had humiliated her by telling her that the sex hadn't meant anything. And that he knew in his heart she wasn't the woman for him.

The memory left a bitter taste in her mouth, even now. She knew that it shouldn't matter to her what Russell did or what he thought, not after the callous way he had treated her. The week before he'd dumped her, he'd played things up with her, being even more romantic, not arguing with her over the little things, and telling her he wanted to surprise her.

She had been surprised, all right. And then she had run out of the restaurant in tears.

There were far better ways to break up with someone. Heck, she would have appreciated a text more. But after dating for two years and talking about moving in together, talking about his plans as a director, and her being there to support his every dream, it had stung for him to—without warning—shatter her world.

Russell was clearly a pig. Even when he had slept with her that one night, he had obviously been involved with Topaz. Which meant he had been cheating on Topaz, as well. The arrogant jerk believed he was God's gift to women.

Nya looked up at Tyler. Gorgeous, tall, sexy as hell… She knew that her kiss with Tyler had gotten to Russell. She'd seen the surprise in his eyes. Russell was the kind of guy who wanted to feel that he had one-upped you and left you devastated.

"It's no doubt he was flaunting Topaz to get to me," Nya muttered, glancing away.

"What was that?"

Nya faced Tyler. "Topaz. I always suspected that she was sleeping with Russell while we were together. And just now she pretty much admitted it."

A look of utter confusion came over Tyler's face, and he shook his head. "Clearly, Russell's missing a few screws." His eyes roamed over Nya from head to toe, leaving her feeling flushed. "For him to dump someone like you…" He made a face.

Nya swallowed. "Thank you," she said. "You're very kind. Why do you even want to do this?"

"I have a sense of adventure," Tyler said. "And I happen to be free on Friday night. Movie premiere, a swanky after party. At least we should be able to have a good time."

Nya regarded Tyler with more than a modicum of suspicion. Did he really want to go to the premiere for the adventure?

Whatever his reasons, it was clear that Tyler was going to insist that they go. And how could Nya insist that they not? After all, she'd brought this situation on herself.

"Okay," Nya said. "We'll do this." And she would play it up for Russell's benefit, because she wanted him to know that he hadn't crushed her forever. Russell would be jealous just thinking about how hot things were with her and Tyler between the sheets.

Oh, he would regret how he had treated her.

"I can pick you up at five, if that works for you," Tyler said. "Take you to dinner first."

Dinner first? The mere suggestion caused Nya's stomach to flutter. Sheesh, this wasn't a real date.

"Why don't you call me at the studio on Thursday?" Nya suggested. But she knew that she would not be going to dinner with him. She didn't want to give him the wrong impression. "On Thursday, I'll be able to have a look at my schedule and make plans then. Sometimes I have to stay late if Sabrina's got a booking."

Tyler nodded. "Sounds like a plan."

"All right." Nya placed her hands on her hips, not sure what to say. "Talk to you later, then." She lifted her drink from the bar, downed the rest of it and walked off in search of Sabrina. She had a headache and wanted to leave.

Chapter 3

The next morning, besides waking up with a headache, Nya was overcome with a profound sense of embarrassment. Had she really kissed a virtual stranger in public last night?

She sat up in bed, and reality settled over her like a wet blanket. No, she hadn't had a nightmare. And she couldn't even claim to have been influenced by alcohol. She had kissed Tyler McKenzie, all right.

"What was I thinking?" she asked herself. It was completely unlike her to have done something so spontaneous and reckless. How foolish of her to try to prove anything to Russell.

"You utter idiot," she mumbled. No wonder Tyler had baited her with the comment that she had been looking for an excuse to kiss *him*. What girl past high school would do something so juvenile to get back at a boy who'd dumped her?

Despite the throbbing pain in her skull and the desire to lie in bed for another couple of hours, Nya threw off the covers and stood. The tile floor was cold beneath her feet, jolting her awake.

She had a mission today. And that mission was to apologize to Tyler and cancel their fake date for Friday night. For some reason, Tyler had pressed the idea of going out with her, perhaps just for the entertainment value of seeing what would happen next. But Nya would not be attending the screening with Tyler or anyone else.

A night of sleep had driven home the point that proving something to Russell simply didn't matter. She was over him, and she had been petty and immature to even try to make a point to him. It was just that she'd been alarmed to see him at the event and had had a knee-jerk reaction. But she was over it now.

Nya showered, which made her feel better. Then she got dressed. Along with her resolve to stop dating and become comfortable being on her own had come a change in attire. Her sexy outfits were in the back of her closet, and she'd opted for jeans and sensible skirts coupled with conservative blouses. Her dresses now went well past the knee and weren't too low at her cleavage.

No point in attracting the wrong kind of attention.

And the flats she wore these days were far more comfortable for her ten-minute walk to the studio than the heels she used to wear. Not to mention the fact that wearing flats had allowed her to walk to work much more, which had contributed to her twelve-pound weight loss over the past few months.

Nya didn't know if Tyler was working at the firehouse today, but luckily Sabrina, who had met sexy firefighter Mason Foley months ago and was still dating him, could relay a message to Tyler. It was Wednesday. There was still time to cancel their date for Friday night.

Nya stopped at a local coffee shop a block over from the studio, where she worked as Sabrina's receptionist and secretary. She got a large cappuccino for herself and a large caramel latte for Sabrina. The single-serve coffee brewer in the studio's kitchen was nice, but there were days when a girl needed something stronger, and this was one of them.

Minutes later, Nya was at the studio. It amazed her that the place looked almost exactly as it had before the fire, only better. Five months ago, fire had raged through the lower half of the studio when Sabrina's father's wife, Marilyn, had thrown a Molotov cocktail through the front window. Consumed with jealousy and anger toward Sabrina, who had been the product of an affair, Marilyn hadn't wanted Sabrina reaching out to her children— Sabrina's half siblings—and had tried to get rid of her. Just last month, Marilyn had pleaded guilty to attempted murder and had been sentenced to fifteen years in prison. She'd been given a lighter sentence for admitting her guilt.

The community had rallied around Sabrina, perhaps in part because of the media attention but also because of Mason's status as a well-respected firefighter. People donated their time and their products and got the studio reconstructed and renovated in four months. The interior now looked better than before, with a more modern feel, new marble flooring and an exit door in the back that would allow for easy escape if there was another fire. Mason had seen to it that the building would never be a possible death trap again.

Sabrina was a workaholic, and Nya was certain that she would find her already in the office. Sabrina lived in an apartment right above the studio, which had largely been untouched by the fire. She was at work earlier and earlier these days, because business had tripled after the firefighter calendar project.

But as busy as Sabrina was, she was definitely making time for love with Mason.

The front door chimes sang as Nya unlocked and

opened the door. It was just before nine-thirty, and the office opened at ten, so Nya left the Closed sign in the window.

"Hey," she called out.

When Sabrina didn't reply, Nya made her way down the hallway that led to the studio in the back. Opening the door, she found Sabrina at her desk in front of her giant Mac computer screen—exactly where Nya expected to see her. Her hair was piled in a loose bun, and she was still wearing her pajamas.

"Morning," Nya said.

Sabrina turned, her eyes registering surprise. Then she pulled the earbuds out of her ears.

"Morning," Sabrina said with a warm smile.

"How long have you been up?"

"I came down just after seven."

"Ouch." Nya winced.

"I've got to get those pictures together from the Miller wedding before they come in later this week."

"You've got time," Nya said.

"Not when more work keeps piling up," Sabrina countered. "If I don't keep on top of it, I'll be buried fast."

Nya walked toward her, extending the cup tray as she did. "Yours is on the right. A large caramel latte with soy milk."

Sighing happily, Sabrina lifted the coffee from the tray. "Thank you. I need this today."

"You're welcome."

Suddenly, Sabrina eyed Nya suspiciously. "Everything okay?"

"Sure. Why wouldn't it be?"

"Well, for one thing, you're bringing me a large latte. You always do that when you want something."

"I'm offended," Nya huffed. And to prove that she

didn't want anything, she changed the subject. "Did you spend the night with Mason at least? Or did you send him home because you had to get up early to get to work?"

"Oh, he was here," Sabrina said, and a smile danced on her lips. "But he had to work at seven. So he was up early. Which worked out, because I needed to be up early, too."

"Good. I'm glad you're not putting work before your man."

"Definitely not. Now that I've found Mason, I'm not about to take him for granted. But it does mean a lot less sleep." Sabrina sipped her latte. "So I definitely appreciate this."

"Nothing like a strong jolt of java to get you started for your day." Nya sipped her own coffee and drew in a deep, satisfied breath. Wow, did she ever need this. Between thinking about the encounter with Russell and the kiss she had planted on Tyler, she hadn't gotten nearly enough sleep.

Wandering around to stand behind Sabrina, Nya looked at the photos on the screen. Once again, Sabrina had captured some elegant photos that this couple would cherish.

"Those are beautiful," Nya said. "Oooh, the ones at the pier… I love them. Especially that one." Nya pointed at the screen. In this particular photo, the bride's veil was flowing in the wind, and the camera had captured it beautifully.

"Thank you."

"You just keep getting better and better," Nya said.

Nya had begun toying with photography in her spare time. But she hadn't dared to tell Sabrina about her newly piqued interest.

"Everyone loved the calendar," Nya went on. "That

picture of Mason, with his chest glistening, was particularly sexy."

Sabrina grinned. "It's possible I put a little more effort into his photos."

"Speaking of Mason," Nya began cautiously, "I do have a favor to ask."

Sabrina flashed her a knowing look. "I knew it! You always bring me my favorite latte when you want something."

"Am I that transparent?"

"Only to me. What do you want? And what could it possibly have to do with Mason?"

Sighing, Nya sank into one of the two chairs opposite Sabrina's desk. "Remember I told you that Russell showed up at the gala last night?"

"How could I forget? He's the reason you left early."

"Well, I need you to talk to Mason. Tell him to tell Tyler McKenzie that the date for Friday night is off."

Sabrina blinked a couple of times as she stared at her with a quizzical expression. "Okay, maybe I need to drink this coffee first, because I'm not making sense of what you're telling me."

Nya sipped her coffee before continuing. "Something happened last night. Something I didn't get a chance to tell you. It's no big deal, and clearly it was just a reaction to seeing Russell."

"Still confused," Sabrina said.

"When I saw Russell last night, he was heading toward me with Topaz. You remember Topaz?"

"The woman he cast in his film. The one you suspected he was sleeping with."

"Yes," Nya said. "Well, seeing Topaz on his arm...I kind of freaked out."

"What does any of this have to do with Tyler?" Sabrina asked.

"Because I did something really stupid. When Russell was walking toward me, with Topaz practically all over him, I panicked. I didn't know what to do, and all I could think about was the last time I'd spoken to Russell and how he'd humiliated me and acted as though I'd never get over him…" Nya knew she was rambling, and Sabrina's look of confusion grew more intense. "I was at the bar to get a drink, and when I saw Russell, I—I just turned to the guy next to me and started kissing him."

"What?" Sabrina's eyes were bulging.

"I know, it was completely crazy."

"Whoa, whoa, whoa, whoa," Sabrina said, holding up a hand. "Are you telling me you kissed someone randomly? Literally just laid one on some guy at the bar? To what? Make a point to Russell?"

"Saying it like that makes me sound incredibly stupid. I wasn't thinking. I just acted. Worst of all, it turns out that the man I kissed was that sexy firefighter, Tyler. He played along with the kiss…perhaps a little too well. Now Tyler and I are supposed to go to the film premiere on Friday night, but I don't want to go. I can't. And that's why I need Mason."

Sabrina drank more coffee. "There are a lot of blanks you're not filling in for me, but that's okay. Let's start from the beginning. What film premiere?" But before Nya could answer, Sabrina continued, "Ohhhh. You mean Russell's film? He finally finished it? And the premiere is on Friday night?"

"Yes. The world premiere is on Friday night, followed by an after party, and he said he wants me there. Probably just to rub his success in my face."

"Why did you say yes if you don't want to?"

"Russell produced two tickets and gave them to Tyler. I tried to decline, but for some reason Tyler told him we'd be there. Probably as a bit of payback for me kissing him the way I did. I didn't want to force the issue and keep refusing when Tyler was pretending to be my boyfriend."

"So you didn't just kiss him. You guys pretended to be a couple."

"There was no plan. As I said, it just happened. But the last thing I want to do is go to Russell's movie premiere, and God only knows why Tyler wants to go. Maybe he actually wants to see the film, or just wants to go for the experience—"

"Or he wants to spend more time with you."

The words caused Nya to swallow her breath and hold it. Did he? He had certainly kissed her back as though he'd been interested, but she had specifically told him to play along. Still, there had been undeniable heat between them as they'd shared that kiss.

Which was exactly why she didn't want to go out with him on Friday night. Not now that she'd sworn off dating.

"I don't want to spend more time with him," Nya said, trying to push the memory of Tyler's mouth out of her mind as she met Sabrina's eyes again. "You know that I've sworn off dating for a year. It's been four months, and I've been going strong with my commitment. I'm not going to waver. So can you please have Mason tell Tyler that I won't be going on Friday night? Considering they work together, it shouldn't be any trouble for him to pass the message along."

"You sure you don't want to go?" Sabrina asked. "Aren't you curious about the film?"

"I can watch it whenever it's released on DVD," Nya said. "I just can't stomach the idea of spending a night watching a project that Russell and I started working on when we were dating. It's not about being hung up on him. It's about not wanting my past to keep invading my personal space."

Sabrina shrugged. "Sure. I'll ask Mason to tell him."

Nya's shoulders drooped with relief. "Thank you."

Sabrina's eyes suddenly bulged. "Oh, heck. I've got to get some clothes on." She jumped to her feet. "And take a quick shower before my ten o'clock appointment.

Nya also stood. "You've got twenty minutes."

As Sabrina hurried out of the studio, Nya inhaled a deep, calming breath. She could finally de-stress. Mason was going to talk to Tyler and cancel the date.

And Nya could get back to enjoying her intentionally single life.

Chapter 4

"So?" Mason began, his eyebrows raised. "What's going on with you and Nya?"

Tyler, Mason and the other firefighters had just returned to the firehouse from a vehicle fire on the Pacific Highway. An SUV had collided with a minivan, and the SUV had caught fire. Thankfully, they'd been able to get the woman and her son out of the car alive, but badly burned. It had been a scene of chaos and fear, after which the mood among the firefighters at Station Two had been dour. So it was an odd time for Mason to be bringing up the subject of Nya.

"Why are you asking me about Nya?" Tyler asked as he began to remove his turnout jacket.

"Sabrina," Mason said. "I just checked my phone, and I missed a call and a text from her. She said she needed to convey an urgent message about your date with Nya on Friday night. Nya wants you to know that she's canceling." Mason flashed him a confused look. "I didn't even know you knew Nya."

Tyler hung his jacket on its hook, then began to take off his boots. So Nya was trying to cancel on him. After all the great points he had made about why they should go to the screening?

Tyler wasn't about to let her off that easily. In fact, all

last night he had remembered the shock—then excitement—when she'd kissed him.

"I met her last night," Tyler said. "Well, I met her *again* I should say. Obviously, I met her when I went to the studio for my shoot."

Tyler felt two strong hands press into his shoulders from behind then heard Omar ask, "Are you talking about that beautiful woman you were kissing last night?"

Mason's eyes widened with surprise. Tyler tried not to show any reaction, though he hated that Omar had blurted that out. But what did Tyler expect? Firefighters were family, and families always teased each other about personal matters.

And when it came to women and dating, Omar was the biggest devil's advocate. He seemed determined to keep some kind of score and to prove to everyone else that he could get any woman he wanted.

Omar had probably been waiting for the right moment to bring up last night's incident, but the morning had been unusually busy with the carbon monoxide call, and now this vehicle fire on the freeway. But Omar had been standing next to him at the bar when Nya had suddenly kissed him. One minute, Omar was pointing out to Tyler a woman that he hoped to go home with. The next, Tyler was making out with Nya in the middle of the bar.

"What about you?" Tyler asked Omar. "Did you hook up with that woman you were checking out?"

"Forget about Omar," Mason said. "He's always getting action. You, on the other hand…you were *kissing* Nya?"

"Hell must have frozen over," one of the other guys said, and a few of them started laughing.

"Very funny, guys," Tyler said, and told himself not to be annoyed. The subject of his love life—or lack thereof—always brought about jokes. Yes, he had stayed with Carol months after their relationship had all but died—and the guys had known it—which was why they acted as though he was completely hung up on his ex. Was it really wrong to have tried to work things out with Carol after investing years with her?

Omar would definitely say yes. Had it been his relationship, he would have left a long time ago and found a new woman to keep him warm.

"You think every time I get some action I come here and gossip about it like a schoolgirl?" Tyler asked. "A real man knows how to keep certain things to himself."

There were some "Ooohs," and another firefighter elbowed Omar in the ribs playfully.

"Hey," Omar began, "I know how much you all enjoy the details. That's why I share."

Tyler turned away from Omar and met Mason's curious gaze. "Did you actually take Nya home for a one-night stand?" he asked, giving Tyler a look that said he would be less surprised if he had been abducted by aliens last night.

"What—you think it couldn't happen?" Tyler countered.

"Hey, if you've finally put Carol in the rearview mirror…" Mason patted him on the shoulder.

"Oh, come on," Tyler protested. "Not the Carol lecture again."

"We wouldn't give you a hard time about Carol if you'd actually date other women," Omar said. "You broke up how long ago?"

Tyler cut his eyes at Omar, who seemed to believe that if he wasn't chasing tail every day, then he was abnormal. Guys like that couldn't understand that it made sense to take some time for yourself after breaking up with a fiancée.

"Four months is not ancient history," Tyler said. "Besides, Carol has nothing to do with the equation. As for Nya," he went on, facing Mason again, "it was quite the interesting experience."

"Tell me you didn't blow it," Omar said.

"Don't you have a morning-after call to make to the woman you were with last night?" Before Omar could respond, Tyler snapped his fingers and said, "Oh, I'm forgetting. You probably didn't even get her name."

There were more "Oohs" and laughter from the guys.

"So you like Nya?" Mason asked, looking hopeful.

Tyler noticed that not only did Mason have a hopeful expression, but so did the other firefighters standing around him, as well. "Since when did my love life become so interesting to you all?"

"What love life?" Omar asked, and laughed.

"We'll see what you have to say on Saturday morning," Tyler retorted. Though his interest in Nya had nothing to do with competing with Omar's scoreboard.

"I don't know about the rest of you," Tyler went on, "but I'm hungry. What's on the menu for today?"

"Fajitas," Mason said.

"Awesome," Tyler said, and began to walk down the hallway that led to the common room. "I'm starving."

In the common room, Omar and the other firefighters headed to the couches surrounding the television. Mason stopped beside Tyler, who had not joined them yet. "So, what am I supposed to tell Sabrina?"

Tyler took a few steps back into the hallway so that he and Mason could have some privacy. "Tell Nya the date's still on."

Mason looked intrigued. "What actually happened last night?"

Tyler told him, and when he was finished with his story, Mason was grinning from ear to ear. "Wow. She just laid one on you like that? That's crazy."

"Tell me about it. But I liked it. Man, she's beautiful. And spunky. I definitely want to see her again."

"All right. I'll tell Sabrina."

"Thanks. Though it's not a real date. Apparently, Nya's ex made a movie, and he invited us to the premiere on Friday night. I told her I'd go with her and continue playing her boyfriend to make sure that her ex knows she's over him."

Mason raised his eyebrows. "And how are you gonna make sure that happens?"

"Look, all I care about is getting to hang out with her again. See where it goes. So I'll be damned if she cancels on me. You make sure to tell Sabrina that the date is still on. No ifs, ands or buts."

"Let's see," Nya said as she perused the calendar on her computer screen. "There's been a cancellation for Friday at 4:45 p.m., so I can get you in then if that works for you. As I said, that's only a last-minute consultation, and you'll have to see if Sabrina will be able to work with you and your schedule."

The woman on the other end of the line thanked Nya profusely.

As Nya hung up the phone, a smile touched her lips. Business certainly was booming. The woman said she was willing to work her date around whenever Sabrina was available. Which spoke volumes about Sabrina's popularity. At this point, Sabrina had bookings well over eighteen months in advance.

It was amazing what a little bit of publicity could do for a business. Nya knew that soon enough, Sabrina might need some help taking photos. It wasn't the reason why she had started tinkering with photography, but she wondered if she could take some classes and get to be good enough where she could be a true partner in the business.

It wasn't something she thought would happen anytime soon, however. She wasn't delusional. But sometime in the future, maybe in a few years, who knew?

Hearing the sound of Sabrina's sandals clicking against the floor, Nya turned to face her as she entered the front reception area. "I just booked you a four forty-five appointment on Friday night. It's just a consultation, and hopefully it won't take more than half an hour. Sorry to book an appointment so late, but the woman was desperate. If you need me to stay, I can go over packages with her and her fiancé."

Nya relished the idea of staying late. Not just because she wanted to become more involved in the business, but also because it would give her the perfect out for her date with Tyler.

Just in case he had given Mason a hard time about it. If he had, now she could honestly say that she had work and didn't think she would have enough time to get ready.

"We'll see how it goes on Friday, but you could always do the consultation if you like. You know the packages I sell, and I'm sure you'll have no problem talking to them about it."

"I do have a feeling that the couple wants to meet you," Nya said. "I can be here to help out, though. And to learn from the best," she added with a smile.

"The truth is, you might not have the time."

Nya stared at her, not understanding. "What do you mean?"

"I have a message for you from Mason. Well, I guess from Tyler, actually."

Nya swallowed. "You do?"

"Mason talked to Tyler, and Tyler told him to tell you that the date is still on. He's not canceling."

"What does he mean he's not canceling? He can't just make an executive decision and expect me to go along."

"Guess he wants to see you again."

"He wants a few laughs at my expense." Nya groaned. "What is wrong with that man? I'm already embarrassed enough by what I did last night. He doesn't have to rub it in."

"I'm kind of surprised you actually don't want to go out with him."

As Nya met her friend's eyes, she knew why Sabrina was confused. Nya had been such a hot mess when it came to men over the past year and a half that she supposed her sudden break from dating was hard to believe.

"I meant it when I said I want to take time to become happy with myself. Ultimately, that's what I was missing when I was dating man after man. I have to be happy with myself. I can't find happiness in the arms of a man."

"Yet you kissed Tyler."

"Because Russell was right there. What was I supposed to do?"

Sabrina eyed her, a hint of amusement on her face. "Not kiss a guy and expect him to *not* want more."

"You think he wants more?" Nya asked, panicked. "Is that what he told Mason?"

Sabrina didn't answer right away, and again Nya felt a sense of panic. Did she see something mischievous in

Sabrina's eyes? Did Sabrina know something and was now trying to gauge her attitude before revealing it?

"Is that what he told Mason?" Nya repeated.

"Relax," Sabrina told her. "Tyler didn't say that. At least that's not what Mason said to me."

"Oh." Nya shuffled uncomfortably in her seat. "Well, that's good." She wondered why she felt the slightest hint of disappointment.

Did she really have to wonder? Obviously, Tyler was hot. She had taken a self-imposed vow of no dating, but that didn't mean that her attraction to men had died. It just meant that she was making sure to watch her behavior, as opposed to reacting spontaneously.

"I don't know, Nya. You're different. It's hard to figure you out. A guy like Tyler… I figured he would be right up your alley."

And he was. Which was the problem. What worried Nya about going out with him was the fact that Tyler was the type of man who could make her forget her vow. And she didn't want to be sidetracked.

"What's to figure out?" Nya asked. "Like I said, I'm taking a break from dating."

"Mason did tell me to tell you that Tyler is one of the good guys."

Nya swallowed. The words intrigued her…and yet she didn't want to be intrigued. "You're not telling me that Mason's trying to play matchmaker now?"

"Just passing along a message. Something to think about."

"Damn, I shouldn't have kissed Tyler. He seriously expects me to go on the date Friday night? Not a date. You know what I mean."

Sabrina gave her another amused look, which irritated Nya. Sabrina was the one who had told her that she needed to slow down when it came to dating. Now it appeared that, just because Sabrina had been bitten by the love bug, she had suddenly lost her objectivity.

"Mason was adamant. He said that Tyler's not letting you out of it. Obviously, no one can force you to go. But why not go?"

"Looks like I don't really have a choice," Nya said glumly. "I used him—shamelessly—so it seems I have to deal with the consequences of my own behavior."

"It's just one evening. And who knows…?"

Nya gaped at Sabrina. "I can't believe you're saying that. You, of all people. You're the one who was forever telling me that I needed to slow down when it came to relationships."

"What can I say? I guess I have a bit of a soft spot for firefighters these days."

A dreamy expression came over Sabrina's face, and Nya knew that her mind had gone to the land of love where she and Mason lived. It was good to see her friend all gushy over a man.

"In fact, Mason and I have a solution to make Friday night not so awkward, if you're concerned about going out with Tyler when you don't really know him."

"What's that?"

"Mason was wondering if you could get two more tickets to the premiere. For us."

Nya's stomach lurched, and she thought she might be sick. "You want me to call Russell and ask him for two more tickets to the event?"

"I'd love to see the film. And hey, if Mason and I are there at the event with you and Tyler, it'll be like four friends getting together."

"Or a double date." The idea mortified her. "You really want to see the film?"

"I was always interested in it when you first started working on it with Russell. So yeah, I'm curious. Besides, it'll be an excuse to dress up and hang out with my man. Get him hot and bothered and then take him home…"

At least Sabrina's words made Nya chuckle. "Wow, Mason really did unleash your inner sex goddess, didn't he?"

"I have to say, I'm happier than I've ever been."

"I believe it."

Sabrina's happy expression morphed into frustration when her stomach grumbled. "And I'm also hungrier than I've ever been," she said. "This has been a crazy morning, but I've got half an hour before my next appointment. I'm gonna run out and get a bite to eat. Think about what I said, okay? Mason and I would love to go to the premiere. If it's not too much trouble for you to contact Russell."

Nya watched her friend disappear through the front door, wondering how things had escalated so much.

The ringing phone distracted Nya from her thoughts, and she got back to work.

Fifteen minutes later, the phone had stopped ringing, so Nya opened up her email. She still knew Russell's email address, as it hadn't been hard to forget. She logged on and typed it in.

Then she paused, not sure what to write.

As the minutes ticked by, she wondered why this was such a hard task. "Get a grip, and get over it."

She drafted Russell an email, asking if two more tickets were available for the event. And as she did, she started to feel better about things. Instead of seeing Friday night as a double date, she started to see it as an opportunity to be with her best friend. Having Sabrina there would lessen the pressure and make it less like a date between her and Tyler. She certainly didn't have to stick by Tyler's side when there were more people there. Tyler could hang with Mason, and she could hang with Sabrina. If Russell was nearby, Nya would make sure to play lovey-dovey with Tyler, but otherwise she could hang with Sabrina.

Yes, it was a great idea to have Sabrina and Mason go along with them. Plus, if she was asking Russell for more tickets, he certainly couldn't believe she was still hung up on him. It was more proof—she hoped, anyway—that she was firmly over him.

Nya sent the message off to Russell as Sabrina breezed back in. She looked harried.

"You really ought to take an hour for yourself. Have a proper lunch, unwind a bit."

Sabrina shook her head as she sipped the last bit of orange juice from a plastic cup. "I don't have the time."

"You know you have to slow down sooner or later. You don't want to disappoint Mason."

Sabrina, who had already passed the reception desk en route to her studio, paused to look over her shoulder. "Oh, Mason's far from disappointed." She winked.

As her friend disappeared, Nya couldn't help feeling a slight sense of wistfulness. Not since Russell had she felt a true electric charge for someone, that sense of excitement and fulfillment that Sabrina was experiencing now.

And despite Nya's resolve to say single, there was a small part of her that still craved that sense of belonging to someone.

There was still a part of her that craved finding Mr. Right.

Chapter 5

"Sabrina Crawford Photography," Nya said into the receiver.

"Nya?" came the male voice.

Nya's heart spasmed at the sound of the deep, sexy voice on the other end of the line. "Speaking."

"Hey, Nya. It's Tyler."

Nya felt a tingle in her belly, which she instantly hated. Why couldn't she turn off her attraction to him?

"Oh, hi," she said, keeping her voice flat. "How are you?"

"I'm great. It's Thursday, so I'm calling to finalize the details for tomorrow as planned."

As planned… He was obviously forgetting that she had tried to cancel the date. But she didn't bother to mention that, saying only, "Right."

"Mason told me that you were able to get two more tickets for him and Sabrina."

"Yep. The more, the merrier, I guess."

"I'm looking forward to it," Tyler said. "I have been all week."

Nya's skin flushed, but she told herself not to read into Tyler's words. First and foremost, tomorrow night was about making it clear to Russell that he hadn't ruined her life forever. Even if Tyler was looking forward to spending more time with her for other reasons, Nya was determined to ignore her attraction to him. She had to change her ways, and not be the same woman she had been for so long.

"If nothing else, it will be an interesting evening," Nya said. "I hope the film is good."

"Mason was saying that we could all maybe meet for a quick bite—if your schedule allows."

"Actually," Nya began, "there's a four forty-five appointment coming in, and I'm not sure when Sabrina and I will get out of here. Might be closer to five thirty, which means dinner will likely not be doable. If the film starts at seven, we've got to be getting there by six thirty to park, get good seats. So we'll have to pass on dinner."

"Good point," Tyler said. "There'll probably be food at the after party, anyway."

"Knowing Russell, he'll have the works."

"Can I pick you up?" Tyler asked. "I think that makes the most sense."

Nya wanted to object, but then she realized she would be protesting too much. What was she going to do—drive to the theater and fight for parking just to make a point? "Sure," she said. "That'll be fine."

"What's your address?"

Nya hesitated, not because she didn't want to give him her address, but because she was suddenly remembering how this story had played out in her past relationships. The guy would pick her up for their date then take her home. Head upstairs with her. It all led to moving too far too fast.

Was she setting herself up for that exact scenario right now?

But she told him her address nonetheless. "I can be downstairs at six fifteen, if that works for you."

"That'll work." Tyler told her. "See you then."

* * *

Later that day, Nya had the firefighters' calendar open to November and the picture of Tyler. Wearing only his turnout pants and suspenders, Tyler was standing in front of the engine truck. One arm was extended above his head and resting on the truck. His magnificent chest was exposed, showing off his muscular pecs and washboard abs. He was one helluva sexy man.

Nya lifted her smartphone and took a picture of the picture.

"Is that the calendar?"

Nya quickly closed the calendar. Then she whirled around to face her friend. "Sabrina. I didn't hear you."

"That's a sexy picture of Tyler," Sabrina said, coming to stand around the front of the reception counter, where she placed her Canon 5D camera. "I thought you weren't interested."

"I—I'm not," Nya stuttered. "I—I was just looking at the calendar again. Checking out your amazing work."

"And you took a picture of Tyler's photo because…?"

"Because…because I told a friend in Texas about him, said he's exactly her type. And she wanted to see a picture."

Sabrina gave her a doubtful look, but didn't press the issue. "Can you please call Dan Silver? Tell him we're going to have to rebook his appointment because I have another appointment in fifteen minutes?"

"Of course."

Sabrina took a moment to stretch her body, leaning backward, then letting her body fall forward. Nya stood and picked up Sabrina's camera. By the time Sabrina was rising and pushing her hair out of her face, Nya snapped a photo of her.

Sabrina threw her a curious gaze. "Hey."

"You're always taking everyone else's picture," Nya said. "It's about time someone took yours."

As Sabrina approached her, Nya checked out the photo on the screen. She'd caught Sabrina in a completely candid moment, and she looked beautiful. Sabrina's hands were in her hair, her eyes gazing ahead. The photo was gorgeous in its simplicity.

"Let me see that," Sabrina said, extending her hand.

"Don't delete the picture," Nya pleaded. "I think you look beautiful."

Sabrina's lips were twisted in doubt as she took the camera. But her eyes quickly filled with wonder, and she actually smiled. "That's a great picture."

Nya smiled proudly. "I told you."

Just as the door chimes sang and a harried-looking man came rushing in, the telephone rang. Nya answered it, and Sabrina tended to the customer.

Once Nya was off the phone, she emailed the photo of Tyler to herself, then accessed it on the computer. Knowing that Sabrina would be busy with the customer for a while, Nya quickly punched in a web address Sabrina knew nothing about.

Within seconds, the pale blue-and-pink swirls on the background of the page loaded, along with the page's logo.

No More Casual Hookups!
Support From Friends Who Care.

Nya had found this site accidentally while on a lark searching the web for support groups for people who were swearing off sex. One night, after a few glasses of wine, she had decided to see whether there were other people out there like her.

Lo and behold, there were. She'd found this support group for people who were renewing vows of celibacy in an effort to find love.

Some were born-again virgins, which of course Nya didn't completely understand. You were either a virgin or you weren't. But she did get the sentiment. Psychologically, they were refreshing their spirits and their sexual beings, saving themselves for marriage.

Nya wasn't saving herself for marriage. Her self-imposed celibacy was about reconnecting with herself, finding joy in her own skin, and escaping from the feeling that she needed to be with a man in order to be happy.

Nya hadn't told Sabrina about this site, because she felt silly about it. There were live chat forums, and there were private messaging options. She'd read some of the forum discussions and had found other people who'd gone through similar experiences. Women and men who had jumped into relationships with hope, only to be hurt. People who wanted to forgo relationships and concentrate on being happy with themselves.

Nya had joined more out of curiosity, because she was surprised that such a group even existed. But she found herself signing on at least once a week to discuss how the week had gone and whether she had been able to withstand the temptation.

Nya had created a username then had started interacting with the group. Even though she'd done so more out of curiosity, she found that they understood her and truly were a source of support for her.

THEONLYWAY, the site's administrator, was logged in. Nya had never come on and *not* found her logged in. While the members didn't give any identifying information about themselves, Nya figured that THEONLYWAY was unemployed, independently wealthy or far too invested in this site to allow herself a personal life.

Within a few seconds of logging in, there were hello messages coming at her from various members who were online. FOOLMEONCE was a male. NOMOREHEART-BREAK, ANDBRAINSTOO and RESPECTME_1 were females.

RESPECTME_1: Hey, MAKING_ACHANGE! How r u?
MAKING_ACHANGE: Feeling stressed. Just need some support from you guys as I'm dealing with an awkward situation.
THEONLYWAY: What's going on?

Nya glanced over her shoulder, fearful that Sabrina might appear. But she knew that Sabrina was busy with her appointment, which would give her the time she needed to get support from her online friends.

Nya loaded the picture of Tyler, then cropped it to obscure his face.

MAKING_ACHANGE: Recently met this guy. Exactly my type. I think he's interested, and I'm afraid I won't be able to resist him.

THEONLYWAY: You want to end up devastated again? That's what will happen if you get involved with this guy. I promise you that.

Nya frowned. THEONLYWAY was hardcore when it came to remaining celibate. For her, the only way to happiness was to abstain from sex until marriage.

RESPECTME_1: No doubt as to why you're tempted! The sexy firefighter? But don't let a hot bod keep you off track! You've been celibate for five months, which is awe-some. Did you sign up for a course in photography yet?

Nya had shared with the group that she was interested in photography, and they'd enthusiastically told her to pursue courses in part to distract herself from dating, but also as a way to find herself and concentrate on her passion.

MAKING_ACHANGE: Not yet. But I plan to. Soon.

NOMOREHEARTBREAK: Be careful! The hot ones al-ways break your heart. L

ANDBRAINSTOO: Yeah, I remember guys like that. Hot and bothered and wanting to get in your pants. Hot guys like that are used to women throwing themselves at them. They're not used to hearing no. I'd stay away!

FOOLMEONCE: Not all attractive guys are heartbreak-ers. But I agree, don't let yourself get sidetracked.

MAKING_ACHANGE: Thx.

RESPECTME_1: Things with Bill are going well. Four months and he hasn't pressured me for sex. Says he's willing to wait.

As the forum members began to write congratulatory responses and supportive messages for RESPECTME_1, who was a born-again virgin saving herself for marriage, Nya shot a glance over her shoulder again. She didn't want Sabrina to catch her in this chat group.

MAKING_ACHANGE: Great to hear, Respect! He sounds like a keeper.

RESPECTME_1: Who knew I'd give up sex and actually find love?

MAKING_ACHANGE: Hate to do this, but I gotta go. At work. TTYL.

As Nya signed out of the chat room, she again felt a little silly that she was even taking love advice from a group of strangers online. She had signed up on a whim, and hadn't truly expected to interact with anyone, much less make any meaningful connections. But she had. She liked these people, even if she didn't truly know them.

Nya was happy for RESPECTME_1, who'd had too many sexual partners and more broken relationships than a person should at the age of twenty-eight. She had decided to swear off sex until marriage—it had apparently worked for her. Nya didn't plan to take her own vow that far, but what she hoped was that the next man she got involved with sexually would be the man she married.

And she held no illusions that that man would be Tyler.

Chapter 6

"What to wear?" Nya asked herself Friday after work as she perused her closet. She had bypassed all of her current outfits and was now searching the back of her closet, where she had discarded her sexier outfits. She needed to look good for the premiere tonight. Only an item from the back of her closet would do.

She almost wondered if she was going to have to run out and buy a new dress when she remembered something she had bought for an event just over a year and a half ago. An event she and Russell had never ended up going to. It was in a garment bag, which was why she hadn't seen it.

She spotted the vibrant red of the dress through the clear plastic square in the garment bag. The dress was stunning. Attention seeking. It hugged her curves, yet had layers of wispy organza that flared from her knees and floated around her ankles.

Nya pulled the garment bag from the back of her closet and laid it on the bed. As she zipped it open, she remembered just how much she loved this dress. It gave her the appearance of having a lush figure, and she remembered how that day in the store she had imagined Russell's reaction when he saw her. She knew he would have been all over her.

She and Russell were supposed to attend some big film soiree in Los Angeles. Nya had bought the dress for that, knowing she would stand out and look amazing.

But Russell had dumped her three weeks before the event.

Nya never had the occasion—nor the desire—to wear it after that.

She lifted the dress and examined the straps made of shimmery crystals. The crystals went across the back of the dress, keeping the material together. The back scooped low, to just above the small of her back, revealing a lot of skin. And the front…it was quite risqué. It was beyond a V-neck. The V plunged nearly to her mid-abdomen, but there was sheer red fabric that connected the material across her cleavage. So the dress was still classy, not trashy. But it certainly oozed sex.

Nya tried on the dress again. She'd lost some weight and wanted to see how it fit her. Looking in the large mirror in the corner of her bedroom, she smiled. Her waist had slimmed down, but thankfully her breasts were still full and filled this beautiful dress in all the right places. Her slimmer waist gave her even more of an hourglass figure now.

She turned, checking out her appearance from behind. She loved how the material flared from the back of her knees. The way the organza flowed around her legs was sheer beauty.

Nya had just the right shoes for this dress. Shoes were her weakness, and she had plenty. She had a pair of dazzling Christian Louboutin shoes with colorful rhinestones that could go with anything. She even had a red purse—not designer—but it matched the shoes perfectly.

She tried on the entire outfit and beamed.

Wow. She looked like a million bucks.

If this dress didn't tell Russell that she had moved on and was having the best sex of her life, nothing would.

When the buzzer went off, Nya jumped to her feet. She scooted across the living room to the intercom.

"Tyler?"

"The one and only," came his reply.

"I'll be down in a moment."

She put her shoes on and fastened them then took one last look at herself in her bedroom mirror. Was that really her? She'd abandoned this beautiful woman months ago. Yes, she knew she was still attractive, but seeing herself dressed to the nines, highlighting all of her body's feminine assets, she almost forgot that this was who she'd once been.

She opted for leaving her hair down, because her efforts to put it into some sort of a sophisticated bun had failed. But she liked the look. Flatironed straight, her hair gave her a decidedly sexy edge. And coupled with her dramatic eyes, including glittery eyeliner and mascara that pumped her lashes thick and long, she knew Russell was going to flip when he saw her.

But she wasn't quite prepared for the look on Tyler's face as she opened the door and stepped onto the front porch. He had been standing beside his white Lincoln MLK, decked out in a suit. The smile gracing his lips morphed into an O the moment he saw her.

His lips parted, and his eyes widened as they roamed over her from head to toe. And when he met her gaze, she could see something brewing in the dark depths of his eyes.

A sense of wonder. And an undeniable look of heat.

He started toward her as she began her descent from

the porch. He hustled, offering her his hand. "Here, let me help you."

Nya took his hand. "Thank you."

Tyler helped her down the front steps, then when she was on the sidewalk, he held her hand high and urged her to twirl.

"Wow." Tyler whistled. "You look… You're stunning."

Nya blushed at the compliment. "Thank you."

"Seriously, I've never seen anyone more beautiful."

Heat spread through her body, and she looked away, not certain she wanted to meet Tyler's gaze. His words alone had left her flushed, because she knew he meant them.

"Has Russell ever had corrective eye surgery?" Tyler asked.

Nya looked at him curiously, not understanding. "Not that I know of."

"Well, he should. Because to let you go, something must be wrong with his vision."

She offered him a small smile then said, "I hope I'm not too dressy."

"You're perfect."

He continued to hold her hand as he carefully led her to his car, as if she were an expensive piece of china he didn't want to break. "I wish I had a limo for you. You look like a movie star."

"Please," Nya said. "Stop."

"Seriously." Tyler opened the passenger door for her. "If your ex doesn't wonder tonight what the heck he was thinking when he dumped you, then I'll have to question his mental stability."

That was Nya's hope. She wanted Russell to acknowledge that she had been special, and that he'd foolishly taken her for granted.

"You're full of compliments," Nya said.

"I mean every word," Tyler told her. Then he closed the passenger door. He cast another glance at her before walking around to the driver's side.

He couldn't get enough of looking at her.

She had looked amazing at the gala, but now…she was beyond stunning. There was no doubt that playing up their fake relationship for Russell's benefit would be an easy task.

In fact, he didn't need Russell to be in the room for him to want to touch Nya. Kiss her. The woman had his libido roaring back to life in a serious way.

Tyler got behind the wheel and started the car. After Mason had told him that Nya had wanted to cancel the date, Tyler had told himself to be detached. That maybe there wasn't the hope of a relationship between them.

But dang, seeing her again…and looking so ravishingly beautiful…he knew that tonight was not the last he wanted to see of her.

Yes, he was having a purely carnal reaction to her. But it was the first one he'd truly had since his breakup with Carol. Attraction wasn't a bad thing. It was required.

And what he was feeling for her now was more than a spark. It was a blaze.

Tyler glanced at her again and swallowed. She looked that incredible.

"I want to thank you again for agreeing to this," Nya said, her voice soft.

"Don't thank me," Tyler said. "The pleasure is all mine."

As he drove toward the theater he hoped that by the end of the night, Russell would be a distant memory in Nya's mind.

And he sincerely hoped that she would be open to creating new memories.

With him.

As they drove down the street nearing the theater, Nya could see a crowd of well-dressed people. She could see the red carpet rolled out to the street and the spotlights lit up alongside it. There were several teams of reporters with video cameras. And she could see at least two photographers snapping photos of the people in the crowd.

"Wow," she said, her stomach fluttering with nerves. "This is a big to-do."

Beside her, Tyler asked, "You okay?"

"Yeah." She faced him and looked into his surprisingly comforting eyes. There was something about him. He was incredibly sexy, yet he didn't have that stuck-up quality that other attractive men did. He seemed earnest and down to earth. Perhaps that was why he went into a field where he helped people.

Tyler pulled up behind a limousine that was in front of the red carpet. "I'm going to let you out here."

"No." Feeling a spurt of panic, Nya looked at him. "I don't want to be here by myself."

"Sweetheart, those shoes aren't meant for walking. I'll park the car, and I'll be right back."

Sweetheart… Did he offer that term of endearment to all women? Or was it a comment on how he was feeling about her?

It doesn't matter, she told herself. *Are you forgetting the advice from the support group earlier?*

They had specifically advised her not to be distracted by a hot body and beautiful face, yet that was exactly what was happening. Just being in the car with Tyler for the drive had Nya's nerve endings tingling with sexual awareness.

"Nya?" Tyler said. "You don't seem okay."

His words pulling her from her thoughts, Nya faced him. "I don't need to get out of the car now. I can handle myself in heels very well." Nya offered him a smile. "Don't worry. I'll walk back with you."

Tyler flashed her a dubious look. "What kind of gentleman would I be if I let you walk a couple of blocks in those heels?" He paused, reached for her hand and gave it a supportive squeeze. "You don't have to be nervous. Russell was a fool to let you go. And the moment he sees you, he's going to know it."

His words made her feel better, and she released a nervous breath. He truly was a gentleman, but she kind of wished he wasn't. Nya could see potential in him, which was only making it harder for her to rein in her attraction.

She glanced away, not wanting to get lost in his dark eyes. That's when she spotted Sabrina exiting Mason's vehicle. "Oh, there's Sabrina."

"Perfect," Tyler said. "Now you won't have to wait alone on the red carpet until I get back from parking the car."

Nya felt waves of relief. "Great, I can wait with Sabrina."

Tyler jumped out of the car then dashed around to her side before she could open the door. A soft smile touched Nya's lips. He was certainly doing his best to be chivalrous.

As he offered her his hand and helped her out of the vehicle, Nya thought about the comments from her friends in the support group. The overwhelming feeling had been that a man like Tyler would use her for his own benefit then leave her in his wake. But she wasn't getting that sense from him at all.

Was he simply on his best behavior tonight? Or was this chivalry an ingrained part of him?

Or was he being extra nice because she looked particularly sexy? Nya had learned a long time ago that men were far more helpful when a woman looked sexier. Something about a woman looking attractive brought out a man's best behavior.

As Tyler led Nya toward the red carpet, she looked around. It took her no more than two seconds to spot Russell. He was near the entrance of the theater doors, speaking to a reporter. He glanced her way, and his eyes grew larger as he took in the sight of her. From what Nya could tell, he also momentarily stopped speaking.

The expression in his eyes was almost the same one she'd seen on Tyler's face. But while Tyler's eyes had widened with wonder and delight, Russell's eyes also held a note of confusion. As though he didn't expect to see her looking so exquisite.

She smiled brightly. Good. It was exactly what she wanted. For Russell to remember what he'd given up when he dumped her.

"Thank you, sweetie," she said to Tyler then eased up to give him a soft kiss on the lips. As their lips connected, she felt a zap of electricity shock her system. She instantly forgot about Russell. The kiss left her slightly disoriented.

Glancing away uncomfortably, Nya pulled her head back. This was a fake date. She had to remember that.

Sabrina looked over her shoulder and caught sight of Nya. Her eyes grew wide, and her jaw hit the carpet. "Oh, my God! That outfit is damning!" Sabrina ran over to her as quickly as she could in her own four-inch heels. She threw her arms around her. "You look incredible!"

Nya eased back, saying, "Thanks. I've actually had this in my closet for a while. This is the outfit I was supposed to wear to that film event in LA with Russell. You remember we were planning to go, but he dumped me a few weeks before?"

"Yes, I remember." Then Sabrina gave her a conspiratorial wink. "Given the way he's looking at you right now, it seems he's remembering just how good he had it before he blew it."

Nya resisted the urge to look in his direction. Instead, she glanced toward the road as Tyler pulled away. Tyler looked at her and smiled. She grinned back.

"Oooh," Sabrina cooed. "What was that?"

"What was what?"

"The look you just gave Tyler."

"I didn't give him a look."

"Nya Lowe, I have known you for years. And you just gave him a *look*."

"I…" Had she? Perhaps she had. But seriously, the man looked exquisite in his tailored black suit and pink tie. And truth be told, it was hard to stop picturing him without his shirt on, like he'd been in that calendar photo. He could so easily drive her to distraction…

"I can't blame you," Sabrina said. "The man is hot."

"Who's hot?" Mason asked.

Sabrina turned and snaked her arms around Mason's waist. "I was just telling Nya that I think she and Tyler would make a gorgeous couple."

"I think they would, too."

"You two!" Nya playfully chastised them. "We are here to watch a movie. To hang out as friends."

"Uh-huh," Sabrina said, flashing her a knowing look. "And that's why you wore that dress."

"I wore this because of Russell," Nya said.

"In part, sure. But you had to know Tyler would look at you and find you irresistible."

Nya's pulse began to race at the mere suggestion. *Did he find her irresistible?*

Oh, who was she kidding? She had seen the smoldering looks he'd given her since he had picked her up. And yes, while she'd known that Russell would flip when he saw her in this outfit, she was also hoping that Tyler would have a similar reaction.

Nya drew in a deep breath and tried to remind herself *not* to be distracted by Tyler. Which proved that she was already losing the battle. How could a person actually turn off their attraction?

And there was something between her and Tyler, a definite chemistry. There was no doubt that if they got together, their physical connection would be explosive. But that was exactly what Nya wanted to avoid. Reacting to her lust. It had led her astray so many times.

Just because there was chemistry between her and Tyler didn't mean she had to act on it. Out with the old Nya, in with the new.

"Nya?"

The sound of her name on Russell's lips had been a question, as though he couldn't quite believe it was her. Nya turned toward him. "Hello, Russell."

"Wow." His eyes were wide, drinking in the sight of her. "You look amazing."

Her back straightened a little as she said, "Thank you." *Now do you feel stupid for dumping me?* she added silently, staring at him with a syrupy smile.

Russell's eyebrows furrowed. "Tyler wasn't able to make it?"

So Russell remembered his name. Maybe no big deal, or maybe it was proof that Russell had lost some sleep over the idea that Nya had moved on with such a hot guy.

"Of course he's here," Nya said. "He's just parking the car. He didn't want me to have to walk far in these heels. Such a gentleman."

Russell turned to face Sabrina and Mason. "Hello, Sabrina."

"Hello," Sabrina said tightly. "Russell, this is Mason. My boyfriend."

"He's also a firefighter," Nya pointed out. "Must be something in the air."

"Or the water," Sabrina added, laughing softly.

Russell was nodding, smiling, but Nya knew him well enough to see that his ego had taken a beating. "You guys should go get your picture taken. I have a photographer here documenting the event. You can get your picture taken in front of the big movie poster, and with any of the cast members, if you like."

"I'll see what Tyler wants to do," Nya said.

Topaz, wearing a sparkly silver dress, walked toward them. As she slipped her arm through Russell's, she shot daggers at Nya. "There you are, babe," she said. "The reporter from San Francisco wants to interview you."

"Ah, I'd better go, then."

Topaz held Nya's gaze for a beat just before she and Russell turned. It was the kind of look that said, *He's mine. Remember that.*

Nya smiled brightly at Topaz, hoping she conveyed her own silent message. *Gimme a break. He's all yours.*

Nya started as strong arms encircled her waist. "Hey," came the deep baritone in her ear.

And good Lord, she shuddered at Tyler's sexy voice. Her reaction to him was purely erotic.

She glanced over her shoulder at him, flustered. Far more flustered than she should be. "Hi. I guess you found a close parking spot."

"Yep. I wanted to get back to you as quickly as possible."

His words made her skin flush, and she looked in Russell's direction. Found him staring at her and Tyler even as he spoke to the reporter.

She looked up into Tyler's eyes, wondering if his actions right now were simply for Russell's benefit—or if Russell was becoming less and less a part of this equation.

Chapter 7

"Well, that was interesting," Nya said as the audience applauded at the end of the film. It hadn't been a masterpiece by any means, but it had been intriguing and at parts quite compelling.

The sex and nudity, however, had been gratuitous. There'd been far too many scenes with Topaz completely naked that didn't add to the story. And the graphic sex scenes would require an NC-17 rating for sure.

"It certainly was," Tyler agreed.

"I don't want to be mean-spirited," Nya said as she stood, "but it's not going to win any awards or anything." She would have handled some of the production elements differently had she still been working on the film. Including the sex. She would have made sure that it was handled in a softer manner that would not turn off any viewers.

"But it was a good effort," she went on. "I did love the gritty quality, the realness of it. I really think it's going to resonate with audiences. Even if there was a bit too much nudity and sex."

Tyler got to his feet, and Nya checked him out as he stretched that gorgeous body. Then he extended his hand to her. "We are going to the party, right?"

Nya looked up at him with a wry smile. "You really were looking forward to this event."

"Not because of the movie or after party," he said, holding her gaze. "But because of the company."

His words made her giddy. It struck her now why she had contacted her online support group earlier. Not simply because she wanted affirmation that she should not pursue a hot guy. But because she knew in her heart that she was fiercely attracted to Tyler, and it was going to take every ounce of her strength to ignore that attraction. That kiss had awakened her repressed desire. And it was her own damn fault.

As she looked at Tyler, saw the undeniable heat in his eyes, she wondered why him, why now? Why had she been so utterly foolish to kiss him? Her life had been going along just fine until then.

Gently, he stroked her face, and Nya actually drew in a sharp intake of breath at his touch. Something about his touch electrified her in a way she hadn't felt in a very long time. What would be so wrong about allowing him in? Allowing herself the possibility of a relationship?

You want to end up devastated again? She remembered the moderator's blunt question.

But as Tyler looped his arm through hers, she wasn't thinking about devastation. She was thinking about how alive she felt.

"Let's head to the after party," he said.

"You bet."

Nya wasn't expecting the extravagantly lavish layout at The Diamond Club for the after party. She had expected something beautiful, but this was above and beyond.

In the center of the room was an elaborate ice sculpture in the shape of a dolphin. Along the far opposite walls, two bars were set up, and waiters wearing black pants, white dress shirts and black bow ties were making their way around the room with flutes of champagne. Some waiters were also carrying trays of hors d'oeuvres.

Cameras were flashing, and the main camera crew that had been front and center on the red carpet was near the ice sculpture, once again interviewing people. Maybe that network was doing a feature story on Russell. It would certainly be great exposure for him.

"Would you like something to drink?"

Nya looked up at Tyler. "I'd love a drink."

"A waiter's coming toward us with some champagne. Will that do? Or would you like something else?"

"Champagne is fine."

Nya continued to survey the room. Beads of glittery crystals hung from the ceiling. A waiter was walking nearby with a platter of shrimp. Another had a platter of beef sliders. Just how much had this cost? It was certainly a lavish party, and Russell must have gotten some serious funding in order to pull it off.

Light jazz music was playing, and a buzz of excited chatter filled the room. Lights outlined a dance floor in the far left corner of the room, near the DJ booth.

"Here you are, beautiful." Tyler handed her a flute then held her gaze.

"To new beginnings," he added, and raised his glass. Then he clinked it against hers.

"To new beginnings."

Both Nya and Tyler sipped their champagne, then Nya glanced to her right. She saw Russell receiving hugs and kisses from people, some of whom had been her friends when she and Russell had been dating. Nya didn't want to go over to him, but there was no doubt that she would have to offer her congratulations, as well.

Turning to Tyler, Nya said, "I guess I should go over to Russell and congratulate him."

"I'll go with you."

He snaked his arm around her waist, and Nya wondered if he felt the heat when their bodies connected.

They walked toward Russell, who had Topaz at his side. The jewelry she was wearing looked like it had cost a fortune. She was certainly giving some of Hollywood's biggest starlets a run for their money.

Russell's eyes widened when he saw Nya, as if he were seeing her for the first time—and as if she were the only woman in the room.

Tyler must have seen the look, as well, because he tightened his arm around her waist. Nya found herself wondering if Tyler was doing that simply for Russell's benefit.

"Nya," Russell said in a singsong voice, stepping away from Topaz and extending his hands to her. He took her hand in both of his. "What did you think?"

"It was great," Nya told him. She offered him a smile as she pulled her hand from his. "Seriously, I'm very impressed." And she was. It still stung a little to know that this was a project she'd started with Russell that she hadn't been able to see through, but she did feel a sense of pride knowing that some of her contributions to the script had remained.

"Russell," Topaz said, a slight edge to her voice. "That executive from Universal just arrived. You should go speak to him."

"Oh, of course." Russell gave Nya a lingering look. "You're ravishing tonight, Nya. It's really good to see you." He glanced at Tyler. "Good to see you, as well."

"Nice to see you. And yes, Nya is ravishing. I feel

like the luckiest guy in the place, because she'll be leaving with me."

Nya's eyes widened. And then Tyler was kissing her cheek and causing heat to flood her entire body. It took her a moment to remember that he was putting on an act for Russell.

"Sweetie," Topaz said. "You really shouldn't keep the executive waiting."

Though Topaz slipped her arm through Russell's, she gave Tyler a look that made Nya wonder if the woman had an agenda to go after every man Nya was involved with. "Tyler," Topaz said, giving him a coy look as she turned to walk away. "Nice to see you again." She didn't even bother to address Nya, and Nya didn't acknowledge her, either. What was the point in pretending? Clearly, they weren't friends.

When Russell and Topaz were gone, Tyler pulled Nya closer to his side and skimmed her temple with his lips. Desire danced along her skin.

"I think he's quite convinced that we're a couple," Nya whispered. "You might have missed your calling as an actor."

"The show's not over yet."

"Hmm?" Nya barely had the question out before Tyler trilled his fingers over her cheek and lowered his lips to hers. Stunned, Nya stiffened. But the moment Tyler's lips touched hers, heat exploded inside her.

His hands caressed her face as his tongue slipped between her lips, and Nya was helpless to step away. Helpless to break the kiss. Instead, she opened her mouth wider, allowing Tyler more access, even though she knew that a kiss like this was completely inappropriate in public.

When Tyler pulled his lips from hers, Nya tipped forward, wanting more. Then, catching herself and realizing just how into the kiss she had been, she took a step backward and cleared her throat.

"Is he looking?" Nya asked.

"Yes." Tyler grinned down at her. "He saw."

"Good," Nya said, hating how breathless she sounded. "I think that was convincing."

"That was nice," Tyler said.

"Get a room, you two."

Nya looked over her shoulder to see Mason grinning at them. Beside him, Sabrina was giving her a wide-eyed stare.

"Excuse me," Nya said, stepping out of Tyler's arms. "I need to go to the ladies' room."

"I'll go with you," Sabrina said.

Sabrina linked arms with Nya as they walked and said, "Are you still going to pretend you're not interested in Tyler?"

"That was for Russell's benefit."

Sabrina scoffed. "So you say. I could *feel* the heat between the two of you."

"We were acting," Nya insisted.

"If you say so."

Half an hour later, the party was in full swing at The Diamond Club. Suddenly Russell went to the DJ booth and took the microphone as an upbeat dance tune came to an end. Russell tapped the microphone.

"Excuse me, everyone. I want to thank you again for coming out tonight to support my film. I'd like to take this moment to thank everybody who's been a part of this project from the beginning."

Nya watched as Russell brought up all of the people

who'd been involved in the film. She didn't even garner an honorable mention.

Sabrina leaned close and whispered, "I can't believe that he didn't even mention you. You were the first one involved in the project."

Nya shrugged. "Oh, well."

"Thank you, thank you," Russell said. He raised a hand to quiet the crowd. "Needless to say, this project would not be the same if it weren't for Topaz Gem. Join me in congratulating her on her performance." Russell began to clap, and others joined. "Topaz," he said as the crowd quieted, "I really appreciate how much you were by my side as I got this project underway. Even before I knew if I would get funding for this film. You believed in this project from the get-go."

Nya's jaw tightened. *She* had been the one who'd been there with Russell from the beginning. The one who had helped him write his grant applications and letters for funding from corporate sponsors.

"I wouldn't have the amazing film I do if you weren't in it," Russell went on. "But more than that…" Russell stopped speaking and lowered onto one knee. A collective gasp erupted among the crowd.

Nya's stomach lurched as Russell reached into his jacket pocket and pulled out a small box.

"Topaz, you're my everything. Without you, I would not have been able to make this incredible film. You've brought so much to my life, and I don't want to move forward without knowing that you're going to be a part of my life forever. Will you marry me and make me the happiest man in the world?"

He opened the box, and Topaz squealed and jumped up and down as she looked at the ring.

"Yes! Yes! Yes!" She dropped down onto her haunches

and kissed Russell on the lips. "Yes, baby, I'll marry you!"

As she kissed him again, this time a longer, more passionate kiss, Nya felt like she could throw up. Russell, the man who had told her that he was not ready for marriage and didn't think he would ever be, had just proposed to Topaz, the woman he'd cheated on her with.

As people were clapping and cheering, Nya turned on her heel and headed for the exit. She pushed through the crowd of people who were smiling as though they'd just witnessed the most romantic moment of their lives.

Nya couldn't stomach another moment of this. She pushed the doors open and ran outside, where she gasped in a deep breath. She didn't know why she was so upset, because she certainly shouldn't be. Russell had proved himself to be a snake, a jerk and someone who was not worth her time. And yet…it was as though he'd staged this event just to humiliate her.

There were people in the room who knew of her commitment to the project long before Topaz had ever come on board. And Russell had deliberately not acknowledged her involvement. Not even in the film's credits. Now, for him to gush over Topaz and propose to her—after he'd made sure to tell her he was not interested in marrying anyone—felt like a big fat slap in the face.

"Nya."

At the sound of her name, Nya turned. Tyler was standing there, a look of worry etched on his handsome face.

"I need to get out of here," she said.

"Because Russell proposed?"

"No, because of everything. Because I shouldn't be here. Because he basically acted as though my involvement in the project never mattered. He's not a part of my life, and he's made sure that I'm not a part of his. And I feel stupid for ever coming here to prove anything to him."

Tyler started toward her, but Nya turned and began to walk down the street. It didn't take long before his hand was coming down on her shoulder. "Hey."

"It's fine, I just need to leave."

He held her in place, and she looked up at him. "You were just going to take off? Leave me there?"

Nya said nothing, because that's exactly what she had planned to do.

"And you say you're not hung up on your ex?"

"Didn't you hear what I said? It's not that. It's just... I feel stupid for having come here. Not to mention that I'm certain that Russell did all of this for my benefit. The jerk."

"So he's still hung up on you?"

"Don't twist my words," Nya said, and shrugged out of Tyler's grasp. "I just don't want to be here anymore. I'll get home on my own."

As she turned to walk away, Tyler said, "Wow."

With a sigh, Nya faced him. "I'm sorry. But please, feel free to enjoy the night with Mason and Sabrina."

"Why are you walking away from me?"

"Because I told you that I didn't want to come to this. I knew it was a bad idea. Yet you insisted."

"So it's my fault?"

Nya groaned. She knew she couldn't entirely blame him as she'd brought this situation on herself. And she didn't want to get into an argument with him. "Please, just stop."

"Nya."

"No," she said, raising a hand. "Just let me go."

And then she whirled around on her heel and began to jog down the street.

Chapter 8

"Nya!" Tyler yelled as he watched her run off down the street. Something inside his gut twisted. He didn't like seeing her in pain, and especially not because of a jerk like Russell.

Tyler watched her for several seconds before deciding to give chase. He wasn't about to let her head off on her own.

He caught up to her easily. "Nya, for God's sake, stop."

He took her by the arm, and she stopped. He turned her to face him and saw that she was crying.

"Damn it, Nya." When he'd insisted on going on this date, Russell had been only an excuse. His only goal had been to spend more time with her. But now she was upset. And he had to take the blame for it.

"Just let me leave."

"Weren't you the one who said that firefighters help people? I'm not about to let you leave and get home on your own when you're this upset. The car's this way. I'll take you home."

Nya brushed the tears from her cheeks as she nodded. "Okay."

"I'm sorry," Tyler said. "I just thought… I thought tonight could be fun. If I'd known you'd get this upset, I never would have insisted that we still go."

Nya hugged her torso. "It's not your fault," she said softly. "I'm the one who kissed you. This whole thing was my mistake."

Her mistake… Tyler's gut tightened. He didn't want her to think of kissing him as a mistake. It had been exactly what he needed in his life.

"Do you want to wait here, or walk with me to the car?" he asked.

"I'll walk with you."

They headed down the sidewalk, and he didn't notice her hobble in her heels at all. Which was good. He didn't want to think that her stubbornness was causing her even more pain.

When they reached his vehicle, Tyler asked, "Are you going to be okay? Do you want me to take you somewhere, maybe get you a bite to eat?"

Nya went to the passenger-side door. "Can you please just unlock the doors?"

Tyler did as she requested.

He noticed that she didn't even glance at him as he got in beside her. He didn't feel good about taking her home and leaving her alone in this condition.

He kept the radio on low as they drove, and intermittently looked in Nya's direction. Her body was leaning against the car door, her head bent against the window. She appeared to be in far too much grief for a woman who was supposedly over a man.

"Hey," Tyler said gently.

"I'm not upset," Nya said, facing him.

"Yeah, you look perfectly all right." Tyler paused. "Word of advice? You've got to move on."

Nya's eyes widened. "You think—you think I haven't moved on?"

"You're a beautiful woman—"

"I'm *humiliated*," Nya stressed. "He proposed to the woman he was cheating on me with—in front of my old friends. He *knew* how that would look. He did it on purpose."

Tyler took her hand. "Okay, so he's a jerk. There's no changing that. Be happy that you're not together anymore. That's all you can do."

"Gee, thanks," Nya quipped, pulling her hand back.

"I'm not being insensitive," Tyler said. "I know what it's like to have to let go of pain." He'd had to let go of his hopes and dreams with Carol when she had suddenly broken off their engagement. After two years of dating and almost a year of being engaged, she'd claimed that they were moving too fast, that she needed to concentrate on her career goals. They'd already been making wedding plans, and Tyler had been the one to cancel all the bookings.

He'd noticed that he and Carol had drifted apart for a good six months. But he'd assumed her focus on opening a business had been a mental distraction. So he hadn't gotten on her case. Instead, he gave her the time and space she needed, always believing she was committed to their relationship. Because once he'd proposed to her, he *had* been committed. He wasn't like his father, who had left his mother at the first sign of trouble.

Nya looked out the window and didn't speak for at least a minute. Then she said, "I gave him yet another chance to get the best of me. That's what hurts."

"When I signed up to play this game with you, I thought it was just that—a game. A bit of fun to get back at your ex. I didn't expect it to end with you in tears."

Neither had she. She felt stupid for even being so upset.

Closing her eyes, Nya forced in a deep breath. Then she tried to evaluate what she was feeling. She had a

bad case of a severely bruised ego. Russell had humiliated her, but she was taking her frustration out on Tyler.

She faced him. "I'm sorry. You don't need to deal with
my emotions right now. I do appreciate you taking me
out. I'm just sorry I couldn't be better company. I feel
stupid for even letting Russell get to me like this. God,
you must think I'm crazy."

He didn't say anything, which solidified for Nya that
he did think she was crazy. And how could she blame
him? Her behavior had been childish. Heck, it even
smacked of a sort of desperation.

No wonder he assumed she wasn't over Russell. That's
how she was behaving. He had hurt her, and for some
reason she had been determined to prove something to
him. On top of it all, she had even entertained the idea
that something might bloom between her and Tyler—
despite her resolve to stop dating.

How crazy the idea had been. And now, there was no
doubt that Tyler would be turned off by her antics.

As if to prove her point, he turned up the radio, making it clear that he didn't want to talk to her. And that was
fine with Nya. After tonight, she would never be seeing
Tyler again. And it was just as well.

This late at night, traffic was light, and it took only
ten minutes for Tyler to get from downtown to her house.
Nya pretty much zoned out and didn't look at him. She
was too ashamed.

There was no doubt that he didn't understand her reaction tonight. But he hadn't known the extent of Russell's
betrayal and how it had affected her life, even now. Nya
had sold her place—and at a loss—because she and Russell had planned to get a place together. And ever since
then, she had been rebuilding her life.

Nya looked at the house where she rented the top floor.

It was far from the luxury home in the hills she and Russell were supposed to be living in.

Tyler pressed the button to unlock the doors, and Nya immediately grabbed the handle. Before she exited, she turned to Tyler and said, "Thank you. And again, I'm sorry for how things turned out."

Then she darted out of the car and hurried up the front steps of the house.

Oh, hell, no, Tyler thought as he watched her flee. She wasn't getting away that easily. The only reason he had gone on this mockery of a date was that, for the first time since Carol, he had felt some serious sparks.

The problem was, she was likely still hung up on her ex. Which meant that pursuing her was guaranteed to bring a whole lot of drama. And yet, Tyler knew that there was something between the two of them. Something worth exploring.

He got out of the car as she was opening her front door. "Nya," he called.

She whipped her head around, the porch light illuminating her wide, expressive eyes. Tyler felt it again, that undeniable pull of attraction toward a woman he had no business being attracted to.

"Tyler, please. I'm already embarrassed enough."

He stalked toward her, his feet moving of their own volition. "Tell me you didn't feel anything."

"What?"

"Tell me you didn't feel anything when we kissed. The first time, or tonight."

"Why are you doing this?"

Tyler hopped up the steps, closing the distance between them. "Why am *I* doing this? Why did *you* kiss me at the fund-raiser? I wasn't the only guy at the bar. Yet you chose me."

"It was coincidence. You were the closest one to me."

"Bull," Tyler said.

"Ty—"

"Tell me you felt nothing," he said. "Tell me you felt nothing, and I'll leave."

Tyler watched her, his breath stopping in his chest. He suddenly realized that he couldn't breathe until he heard her response. If she told him that she'd felt nothing…

But she didn't. Instead, she sighed in frustration and turned back to the door.

Vindicated, Tyler placed a hand on her shoulder and turned her. Then he placed a finger under her chin and forced her to look at him.

Slowly, Nya met his gaze, her eyes glistening beneath the house lights. Damn, she looked so darn kissable.

So irresistible.

Tyler slipped his hand around her waist and pulled her against him. A soft sigh escaped her as her body landed against his. The feel of those breasts against his chest… he wanted her.

"Seems you need me to kiss you again to give me an answer." He paused and ran the pad of his thumb over her bottom lip. "So I'm going to do that. And then I want an answer."

Tyler heard the softest sound of breath escape Nya's lips. He didn't know if it was an invitation, or if she had been about to mumble a protest. Then his lips came down on hers, and the fiery passion that ignited between them was undeniable.

Her lips were still at first, as was her entire body. He moved his lips slowly over hers, coaxing her into surrender. He wanted to feel that moment when her shoulders loosened, and she gave herself completely to the kiss.

He didn't have to wait long. Within a few moments the most heavenly moan slipped from Nya's mouth. Her body softened against his, and she snaked her arms around his neck.

Tyler's tongue slipped into the warm recesses of her mouth, and he could taste a hint of champagne on her tongue. It made him delirious with need.

He stroked her face as he kissed her, and suddenly Nya was kissing him back with ferocity. Her fingers dug into his skin at the nape of his neck as if she was trying to hold on for dear life. And maybe she was. Because Tyler felt the same way. That holding her right now was critical to his entire existence.

He needed to have her in his bed.

Tyler broke the kiss, and he heard Nya's soft moan of protest. He stared down at her, into her eyes that were now darkened with desire. "You felt something," he said after a moment, remembering why he had even kissed her. "There's no need to state the obvious." He trailed a finger along her cheek as he still held that lust-filled gaze then trailed his finger down to the area above her bosom. "There's something between us. You know it, and I do. But what I need to know is if you're still hung up on your ex—"

"I'm not," Nya rasped. "If I never see him again, it will be too soon."

"Good." With a growl, Tyler drew her against his body and planted his mouth on hers again. He thrust his tongue between her lips, and she opened her mouth for him, giving him the access he craved.

The kiss deepened, making Tyler hot and hard with a need that he hadn't felt in a long time. Gripping her behind, he pulled her against his groin. Moaning, Nya curled a leg around his calf. And damn if those moans weren't making him absolutely mad with lust. He lifted her, and she tightened her arms around his neck and wrapped her legs around his waist.

Tyler wanted nothing more than to take her right here.

"I need to take you to bed," Tyler said. He was surprised by the words that were coming from his mouth. It wasn't a question. He wasn't giving her the option to turn him down.

Tyler kissed the underside of her jaw then whispered, "Don't say no."

"I— This is wrong."

The words were like a stab in the gut. "Nya…"

Her chest was suddenly heaving. "I—I can't get sidetracked by you o-or anybody else."

"What?"

"You look nice, you seem nice, but no." She jerked backward. "I—I can't."

"Talk to me, Nya."

"Maybe if I met you later."

Tyler stared at her in confusion. "Met me later?"

She turned away from him, opened the door and darted inside. Without looking over her shoulder, she said, "Goodbye, Tyler."

She closed the door, and Tyler stared at it, stupefied.

And then he heard her scream.

Chapter 9

Nya flailed as she tumbled backward down the stairs. She finally came to a hard stop on the bottom landing. In her haste to get up to her apartment, she had twisted her ankle in her four-inch heels.

The door flung open. Nya saw Tyler enter the small foyer, his tall, strong body seeming to fill the entire space. It took him only a moment to see her in the darkened room, and he quickly ran to her side. He stooped down and pulled her into his arms.

"Nya, damn it."

Tyler sounded both worried and disappointed at the same time.

Nya turned away from him and softly began to cry. Not so much because she was hurt—although her ankle was throbbing. But mostly because she was yet again humiliated. She was stressed, embarrassed, upset with herself for her behavior tonight. Could this night get any worse?

"Tyler, please."

"Don't send me away again. I need to see if you're okay."

"I could die of embarrassment, but I think I'll live."

Tyler looked into her eyes. She saw compassion there, which touched her in a way that she didn't want to be touched. She wanted him to be a jerk. She wanted to see a side to him that she didn't like. It would make it all the more easy for her to reject him.

"Where's the light?" Tyler asked.

"It's on the wall. Right behind you."

Nya thought that Tyler would release her as he went to turn on the light, but instead, he gathered her into his arms and stood. Instinctively, she put her arms around his neck and held on. He was strong and lifted her as though she weighed no more than a few pounds. She had to admit that there was something so darn sexy about being in the arms of a strong and sexy firefighter.

He turned on the light, and she was even more embarrassed. Because she didn't want him to see her this way. She wasn't herself. "You can put me down," she told him. "I'll be okay."

"I told you those shoes were dangerous." He paused then said, "Are you so desperate to get away from me that you end up hurtling yourself down the stairs?"

Nya didn't know what to say. Because that was exactly what had happened. She'd started to run away as though he were some demon chasing her, and in her rush, she had fallen.

And now here he was again.

"Your place is upstairs, I take it?" Tyler asked.

"Yes. I rent the upstairs level."

Without further question, Tyler started up the stairs. And as he did, Nya allowed herself a moment to simply enjoy the feeling of being in his arms. He was strong— and he was taking care of her. How long had it been since she'd had a man take care of her?

But she didn't want him to think she was a fragile, pathetic girl. So when they got to the top landing, she said, "You can let me down. Thank you."

"Not yet. I'm going to see you into your apartment. Make sure that you're okay."

Tyler's words left no room for dispute, so Nya didn't argue. Instead, she handed him her key, and he maneuvered his body and opened the door while still holding her. He stepped inside and found the light switch.

"The place is a mess, I'm sorry."

"I don't care what your place looks like." Tyler started toward her living room sofa, and once there he said, "I'm going to ease you down. Tell me how your foot feels, if you can put any pressure on it."

He started to lower her, and she put her right foot on the floor and tried to put pressure on it. "Ow!" Her knee buckled as she felt pain shoot through her injured ankle. Tyler slipped his arms around her, and she eased into him. "Looks like you've sprained your ankle."

"I'll live."

"Or it could be a strain. I want to have a look at it. Hopefully, I can determine if it's anything worse than a simple strain."

"Tyler, is this really necessary? I twisted my ankle. I'm going to be fine."

He sat on the sofa and pulled her onto his lap. She landed against his body with an *oomph* and felt a jolt of sexual awakening as her bottom came onto his lap. Then he quickly slid her off him and to his side, and took her foot in his hands. "It's the right foot, right?"

"Yes."

He undid the straps on her expensive shoe, and pulled her foot out. Nya noticed how he treated her with extreme gentleness.

"Do you have paramedic training?" she asked.

"Yep," Tyler told her. "Can you wiggle your toes?"

She began to wiggle them and was surprised at the amount of pain. "I can, but it hurts a little."

Tyler felt gently around her ankle. "I can already see some swelling." He took her foot in his hand and gently moved it inward, toward her other leg. "Does this hurt?"

"Not so much."

"What about this?" He angled her foot the other way.

"Ouch!"

"That must be the way you fell. It looks like your ankle rolled to the left."

"I was heading upstairs, and I lost my footing in the shoes."

"You were running. Running away from me." Then he looked at her, and she could see the frustration in his eyes. "Why did you feel the need to bolt like that? Did you think I was going to hurt you?"

Nya didn't know what to say. One minute, she and Tyler had been caught in a heated kiss. The next, she'd wanted nothing more than to get naked with him. And somehow, that realization had registered in her brain and raised a warning flag. Reminded her that she had been about to do the same old thing she had done in the past.

Move too quickly with someone she liked.

"The truth?" she asked. "I had to put the brakes on."

"Because of Russell?"

"Please—stop saying that it's because of Russell. I never want to hear his name again."

"What do you expect me to think?" Tyler asked. "We were at the party, he proposes to another woman, and you lose it."

"I'm frazzled. Stressed. Russell told me a lot of things, and I guess seeing him there tonight and hearing him *not* acknowledge my work on the film then gush over Topaz the way he did… I realize how foolish I was to believe everything he said to me." She paused and held his gaze for a beat. "I used to own a condo. I sold it at a loss because Russell and I were supposed to move in together. Then he dumped me. So it's not just the fact that we're not together. It's that he sold me all these lies, and I believed them." She blew out a frustrated breath. "I've told myself over the past several months that I can't let myself be fooled by anyone else." She met his eyes, held his gaze.

"So you think I'm going to fool you?"

"I—I'm not saying you're not a perfectly nice guy."

"But you don't want to give me a chance because of Russell."

"It's not about Russell. And it's not about you. I guess… It's about me. You put me on the spot, asking me if I was attracted to you. And…I felt uncomfortable."

Nya saw the look of surprise in Tyler's eyes. Perhaps even a little hurt. "I would never force you to do anything you don't want to do," Tyler said. "I have no interest in hurting you. I thought…I thought we were both on the same page."

Nya said nothing, but she felt a little guilty. She *had* been into it. More than she should have been. Her running away from him had everything to do with needing to maintain her own wits, and nothing to do with rejecting him.

Because she wanted him. There was no doubt about that.

"We were on the same page," she admitted. "But then… I just… I wanted saner heads to prevail." She groaned softly. Perhaps she was making no sense. Perhaps he didn't understand.

"For the record, I'm not at all like Russell. He sounds like a real jerk. He took you for granted, and I'm sorry you had to go through that."

"It's been a long night," Nya said. "I think all I really need right now is a good night's sleep. I feel foolish that you're up here, that you're tending to me like a baby..."

"Do you have any bandages?" Tyler asked.

"What do you mean?"

"Something to wrap your ankle with. I think it's just a strain, nothing more serious than that. I doubt there's a hairline fracture or anything."

"You think I could get a hairline fracture from a little tumble down the stairs?"

"I've seen the most innocuous falls result in serious brain injuries, even death. You can't take anything for granted. But I think you'll be fine. Make sure to keep your foot elevated to keep the swelling down."

"Can I go to work?" Nya asked, and offered him a soft smile. She was hoping to add a little levity to the situation, especially after her behavior.

"You work on Saturdays?"

"Yes," Nya said. "Sabrina has bookings on Saturdays and even Sundays."

"I'm sure you'll be fine by Monday. But my recommendation is that you wear flat shoes," he added, returning her smile.

Nya chuckled softly. "Honestly, I feel really silly that you're here. I can take care of myself."

He looked at her, but said nothing, and she got the feeling that he wanted to retort, *You could've fooled me.*

"So do you have any bandages?"

"Sorry, I've got nothing."

Tyler eased himself up from the sofa and gently put her leg there. "Hold on a sec."

She watched him make his way to her kitchen and heard him opening the fridge and drawers. A minute later, he was back with ice in a plastic bag in one hand

and a dish towel in his other hand. He put the ice into the dish towel and brought it to her leg.

He picked up one of the decorative cushions on her plush sofa and put it underneath her foot to elevate it. Then he placed the ice bag on top of her ankle. "Hold this in place for ten minutes until I get back."

"Until you get back?"

"I'm going to a drugstore to get something to wrap your ankle with."

"That's not necessary," Nya protested.

"Your ankle needs to be wrapped. I'm going to do it for you. I'll be back as soon as I can."

As Tyler left the apartment, Nya stared at his back with a sense of confusion. Why was he even bothering with her? Hadn't she shown herself to be irrational and overly emotional?

When he returned, Nya had changed into pajamas. She'd had to hobble around a little bit. The pain in her ankle was greater than she had expected. When Tyler opened the door, he found her on her feet near her bedroom. He took one look at her in her pajamas and frowned. "Did you keep your foot up at all?"

"I did…for about five minutes. But then I figured I needed to get changed, and I had to brush my teeth."

Tyler shook his head. "You're stubborn, aren't you?"

"Just used to taking care of myself," she told him.

"Well," he said, approaching her, "tonight I'm going to take care of you."

"Tyler, I'm not an invalid."

"I didn't say you were." Nonetheless, he lifted her into his arms.

"Tyler!"

He carried her to the sofa where he gently put her down then sat beside her and pulled her injured foot onto his lap. Nya watched as he took out the bandage. He had taken off his jacket, and Nya assumed he had left it in his vehicle. Now she could see the breadth of his wide shoulders beneath his white dress shirt. She could see those muscular biceps. It struck her anew that this gorgeous man was in her apartment taking care of her.

The last time she'd had a gorgeous man in her apartment, they had quickly gotten naked. She couldn't imagine that that guy would have taken the time to nurse her if she'd been hurt in any way.

Tyler gently began to wrap her ankle.

"Looks like it'll be flip-flops for me tomorrow."

"Where are you going tomorrow?"

"Oh, I just have some shopping to do. I need some groceries."

"You have shoes with a bit of support? Not so flat, I mean?"

Nya nodded. "Sure."

"Good." Tyler finished the job then rubbed her leg above her ankle. "How are you feeling now?"

"I'm okay. Just…like I said before, embarrassed."

"How does your head feel?"

"Huh?"

"Did you hit your head when you fell? I didn't even ask you that."

"I don't think so." Nya shrugged. "I don't know."

"I think I should stay for the night," he announced. "In case you suddenly feel odd. I want to be here on the off chance that you develop further symptoms."

Stay the night? Nya's heart began to accelerate. "What? B-but I'm fine."

"I'm not convinced that you don't have a concussion. I'll feel better if I stay here with you, and make sure that you're okay."

Nya's heart was pounding at an unhealthy rate. The idea that Tyler wanted to stay the night…was this his way to get into her bed? Play the nice guy then ultimately get her naked?

Tyler got up from the sofa then picked her up again. He began carrying her toward her bedroom.

"What are you doing?" Nya asked.

"I'm taking you to bed."

Nya's eyes widened in alarm. "What? Didn't you hear everything I said earlier?"

"Relax, sweetheart. I'm going to *put* you to bed. Not have my wicked way with you."

Have my wicked way with you… The words caused her body to tighten with sexual anticipation. And she actually felt a wave of disappointment, knowing that Tyler *wasn't* going to ravage her body.

But wasn't that exactly what she wanted? For there to be *no* sex tonight?

Rationally, she knew that she should *not* engage in a sexual relationship with Tyler tonight.

But emotionally…oh, how nice it would be to give in to temptation…

In the room, Tyler placed her in her bed. He took one of the throw pillows that was at the side of the bed and put it beneath her foot. Then he pulled the sheet over her. "You feel comfortable?"

She felt more than comfortable. She felt slightly aroused, sexually frustrated and embarrassed. "Yes. I'm good."

Tyler glanced around her room then began walking toward her dresser. He lifted the Nikon camera then looked at her. "Hey, what's this?"

"It's a camera."

"Obviously," Tyler said. "I didn't know you were doing some of the photography at the studio."

"Oh, no, I'm definitely not," Nya said.

Tyler stared at her, confused. "You make it sound like the idea is crazy." He lifted the camera in front of his face. "But you have an expensive camera like this? It tells me you're interested in photography."

"I'm not. Not really."

Tyler eyed her suspiciously. "So you're interested in photography, but you don't think you can do it."

Nya drew in a startled breath. How had he so easily summed up her exact issue? She said nothing.

"Does Sabrina even know?"

"No!" Nya said, sounding more panicked than she should. "Look, it's just…just a hobby."

Tyler fiddled with the camera, and Nya heard it turn on. Then, coming closer to her, he said, "Say cheese."

"Tyler—"

He snapped a photo. "Oh, my God. You have to delete that."

"Smile," Tyler insisted.

Knowing that she could delete the photos later, Nya forced a smile. Tyler took another picture.

"Beautiful," he said as he checked it out in the viewfinder.

"Will you please put the camera down now?"

Tyler did as she instructed. Then he walked toward the bedroom door, where he turned off the light before leaving the room.

Expelling a relieved breath, Nya closed her eyes. Thank God he was out of her room. Though she had no clue how she was going to sleep knowing that Tyler was outside her bedroom

When she heard the door open a minute later, Nya's

eyes flew open. Alarm shot through her body like a jolt of electricity.

Tyler was clad only in white boxer briefs. The streetlight spilling in through the blinds showed that he was nearly naked.

And that he had a phenomenal body. Oh, dear Lord. He had the most amazing muscular thighs! Not to mention that chest and those arms.

He began to approach the bed, and every one of Nya's nerve endings was on edge. "Wh-what are you doing?"

"I'm going to lie down with you. It's better for me to monitor or hear if anything goes wrong in the night. If you have a blanket, I'll make myself comfortable on your armchair."

Nya could hear her pulse roaring in her ears. "B-but… you're…where are your clothes?"

"I can't very well sleep in my suit."

"You—you want to sleep in my room?"

"It's the best way for me to monitor you."

"I—I'm fine."

"I want to be sure."

Please, God, tell me this isn't happening.

"Where's your linen closet?"

"In the hallway," Nya said, her heart thundering in her chest. The idea of Tyler sleeping in her room was throwing her for a loop.

He exited the room and returned a minute later with a comforter. Then Nya watched as he tried to get comfortable on the armchair, which was far too small for his body. She knew what she had to do.

"There's plenty of room in my bed," she found herself saying. "If you really think it's necessary to…to monitor me."

"I'll be fine right here," he told her.

"No, you won't. Your body will be cramped in the morning, and I'll feel guilty." She exhaled a harried breath. "You can share my bed, Tyler. Just as long as respect that there will be no sexual activity."

When he didn't get up from the chair, Nya tossed the pillows from the left side of her bed onto the floor and threw back the covers beside her.

Finally, Tyler made his way over to her. A breath snagged in her chest as he climbed into the bed beside her.

This was really happening. He was actually going to sleep *in her bed*? God help her, how was she going to be able to resist him?

Perhaps he saw the panicked look on her face despite her offering him the bed. Because he then said, "It's okay. I heard everything you said earlier. You don't have to worry, Nya. You're safe with me."

Chapter 10

A crowd of people were lining the sidewalks and spilling into the road. Frantic hands waved to get their attention as they pulled up in front of the restaurant on Pacific Bay Street. There was no need for anyone to point out where the fire was. All of the firefighters could see the flames shooting out of the back of the restaurant.

Tyler parked the pump truck, and then he and all of the firefighters jumped out and got to work. As the engineer, Tyler quickly went to the back of the truck and started disassembling the hoses. He dragged the main hose and attached it to the fire hydrant. He then returned to the back of the truck to use the pump controls to turn on the water and adjust the pressure levels of the various hoses that the firefighters would use to attack the flames.

The fire station's chief, Tom Sully, was out of his vehicle and barking commands. "Ewing," he said, referring to Lieutenant Omar Ewing of the ladder truck. "Get that ladder extended to the top of the building and open up a hole in that roof before any of our men go inside."

Tyler continued to get the hoses ready as the ladder was extended to attack the fire from the top of the structure. Mason, captain of the engine truck, took a hose and along with Clive Jennings, went to the front of the building to begin spraying water.

Tyler watched as Omar and Wyatt, two firefighters from the ladder truck, climbed the ladder and got onto the roof. It was important to put a hole in the structure to avoid any backdraft when the firefighters tried to enter the building below.

The flames were shooting high into the sky, and there was the risk that the fire would jump to its neighboring buildings if they didn't get it under control—fast. Had gasoline been used as an accelerant to cause the fire to spread rapidly?

"Is there anybody inside?" the chief asked. There was pandemonium and chaos, but Tyler could hear from the witnesses on the street that no one was inside the restaurant. There'd been an explosion in the back, and all of the patrons had managed to run out to safety. Four of the restaurant staff had been hurt, including two chefs. One of them was sitting on the curb in front of the restaurant, the arm of his white outfit burned. A female chef, also in a white outfit, sat beside him. Her face appeared to be covered in soot. Both of them looked dazed and disoriented, and a paramedic team was now tending to them.

A good couple of dozen people, both restaurant staff and patrons, were hugging each other, crying and watching the fire with a sense of disbelief.

Tyler wondered how long it would be before people feared going out for dinner. After the second restaurant fire, people in Ocean City had been certain that a serial arsonist was on the loose, taking pleasure from burning down restaurants. Establishments that hard-working citizens had put their time, money and hearts into.

This was personal for all of the firefighters in the city. Arson left lives destroyed. Sometimes people were horribly injured and would have to deal with the consequences for the rest of their lives. Sometimes people were killed, which left families shattered. Tyler knew that each and every firefighter in the city was determined to see this deranged arsonist caught.

Nearly an hour later, the blaze was under control. The entire time, people watched on the streets. When the danger had finally passed, a woman in her midforties whose eyes were swollen from crying came over to Tyler at the back of the pump truck. "It's that arsonist, isn't it?"

"I can't say for sure, ma'am."

"We only opened last month," the woman went on, letting Tyler know that she was one of the owners. "We put our whole life savings into this." The woman brushed her tears away. "Why haven't you guys caught who is doing this?"

Tyler felt for her. He knew that she was frustrated, and he also understood that her frustration was not truly directed toward the firefighters. It was devastating to see your hard work go up in flames in an instant. She was desperate for answers, and so far there were none.

Tyler knew how she felt. He still wished there were answers as to why his childhood best friend had burned to death in a house fire. It was the loss of his friend at the tender age of nine that had caused Tyler to choose the profession of a firefighter.

"I assure you, the fire department and the police department are doing their best to solve this—and quickly. We know how devastating this is to everyone in the city, including us. We all like to go out and eat. And we're going to do our best to make sure that this arsonist doesn't continue to take away the joys we're all entitled to in this city."

A man came over to the woman and put his arm around her shoulder. Tyler assumed the man was her husband. "I can't believe this," the man said. "We opened up this restaurant with a strong ethical sense. We only use free-range, locally raised animals. Who would want to hurt us?"

Tyler knew that the man had asked a rhetorical question, and didn't expect a response from him.

"We didn't even get a threatening letter," the man went on. "I thought all the victims of the arsonist were getting letters."

"I assure you, the investigation is ongoing," Tyler said. Yes, the first four victims had been sent threatening letters. But maybe the arsonist was changing. Maybe he wanted every restaurant owner on edge. "I'm sorry this happened to your restaurant," Tyler added.

The man nodded, then pulled the woman tight against his side. Together they walked off, continually glancing up at the shell of the building that had once been their restaurant. Smoke was still smoldering, but the blaze was now under control.

However, Tyler knew that would be little comfort to them. Hopefully, they had insurance. But it would be months before they could open their doors for business again. They might even be so devastated by this fire that they would ultimately sell.

Mason walked over to Tyler, removing his face mask as he did. Now that the blaze was under control, the firefighters were desperate to get water and cool off. Mason dipped his face into this spray of water that Tyler offered to the firefighters who were coming up to him.

"Another arson," Tyler said.

Mason looked at him, anger brewing in his eyes. "This has to stop."

Tyler looked through the crowd, an idea suddenly coming to him. It was very common for perpetrators of such crimes to become a part of the audience, to get a kick out of watching their handiwork.

He scanned the crowd and saw eyes that expressed worry and concern. Until he met the gaze of a man in a red ball cap. These eyes were different. They didn't express compassion. They expressed a sense of wonder.

The man held Tyler's gaze for a beat, and Tyler got an unsettling feeling.

"Mason," Tyler said, turning to look at him. "The guy across the street with the red baseball cap." By the time to Tyler looked back across the street, the man was disappearing into the crowd.

"Hey!" Tyler said, starting across the street.

"What?" Omar asked.

"That guy," Tyler said, throwing a glance over his shoulder at Omar and Mason. "The one with the red baseball cap." It wasn't a coincidence that Tyler had made eye contact with him, and now the man was fleeing through the crowd. "We need to get to him. I think he may be the arsonist."

Both Mason and Omar started across the street with Tyler, and then Tyler began to jog. But the man had quickly darted down the alley. By the time Tyler got to the mouth of the alley, the man was nowhere in sight.

"Dammit!" Tyler had been staring at the arsonist. He was certain of it.

But he had gotten away.

"Did you get a good look at him?" Omar asked. "Because I didn't."

"Not really," Tyler admitted, and then blew out a frustrated breath. "He wasn't that close, the people around him obscured much of his face. But I saw his eyes. All I can tell you is that he's a white male, dark hair."

"He was wearing jeans, a black T-shirt," Mason added. "Looked about five-foot-eleven. Pretty nondescript."

"Dammit," Tyler repeated. "If only I'd noticed him sooner."

But those eyes… Tyler was fairly certain that if he saw the guy again, he would be able to recognize those eyes.

It just meant being patient. Because Tyler was certain that he would strike again.

Nya reread the note for the third time, a small smile lifting the corners of her lips.

Nya, you seemed okay during the night. You slept soundly, and my prognosis is that you're going to be okay. :) Sorry I had to leave, but I've got to get to work. Make sure you keep that foot elevated. Take care.
PS: I told you that you could trust me.

Nya sighed happily then stretched her body from the sofa to place the note on the coffee table. She couldn't believe that Tyler had been at her house and slept in her bed with her, yet nothing had happened.

And it endeared her to him all the more. She had slept, but not for a long while. Not until she'd heard Tyler's own heavy breathing and had been certain that he was asleep. Despite his words that she could trust him, she had wondered if he was going to eventually make a move on her.

A part of her was expecting that he would and feared that if he made an advance, she would not be able to turn him down. After all, the guy was seriously hot.

She knew how this game was played.

But Tyler had been a man of his word, and it lifted her spirits to know that he wasn't the type of guy to lie to her. To lure her into a false sense of security and then make his move.

Clearly, he had wanted to make love to her. And she had given him every reason to believe that she wanted the same. So the fact that he had had enough respect for her to not push a different agenda meant a lot to her.

It made her want to see him even more.

Nya lifted her laptop from the coffee table and turned it on. She immediately went to the website for her support group and logged in so that she could chat. She found only two of the people she normally corresponded with online. THEONLYWAY and ANDBRAINSTOO.

MAKING_ACHANGE: Hi!

Both of the other women responded with cheerful greetings, complete with emoticons of happy faces and hearts.

MAKING_ACHANGE: Well, had an interesting night.

THEONLYWAY: What happened?

MAKING_ACHANGE: Remember that firefighter? I went out to an event with him, and it turns out he's a total gentleman. He took me home, and I worried he was going to make a play for me. Long story short, I hurt myself, and he had to help me. He insisted on staying the night to make sure I was okay. I totally feared I would give in to him if he made an advance. But he was a gentleman. He took care of me, and even left before I woke up.

ANDBRAINSTOO: Aww, that's sweet.

THEONLYWAY: You shouldn't have had him go to your place. That was foolish!

MAKING_ACHANGE: I know, but…the good thing is, he respected me… I feel like he passed a test.

THEONLYWAY: Why are you putting yourself in a vulnerable position? You should not be dating now. Remember, you made a pledge of celibacy for a year.

Nya frowned. Yes, she had. But it wasn't like it was written in stone. She could change her mind at any time. And besides, her virtue had remained intact. Wasn't that the point here?

ANDBRAINSTOO: There are still some good ones out there.

MAKING_ACHANGE: That's what he proved to me. :) Gives me some hope. And you know what? It was nice having someone here to take care of me. That's one of the things I miss about not being in a relationship.

THEONLYWAY: You are a strong and confident woman! You don't need anyone to take care of you!

The doorbell rang, and Nya looked over her shoulder. It was just after eleven on Saturday morning. Who was here?

She limped over to her intercom and pressed the buzzer. "Hello?"

"Nya, it's Tyler."

Nya's heart began to pound. Tyler was here? "I thought you were working today."

"I am. So I only have a minute. Can I come up?"

Nya hesitated. How could he come up when she barely looked decent?

"I don't understand. If you're working, how are you here?"

"All will be revealed if you let me up."

Tyler had seen her at her emotional worst last night. So what if her hair wasn't done, and she wasn't wearing any makeup?

She pressed the buzzer to release the door then made quick work of fluffing her hair with her fingers. It was all that she could do.

Moments later, there was a knock at the door. Nya took a deep breath then opened it. And there stood Tyler in his firefighting outfit, looking so…heroic. He truly was gorgeous. Whether he was wearing a tuxedo or his fire-retardant suit, he looked incredible.

"Hi," Nya said softly.

He grinned down at her. "Hey."

"I wish you'd given me some notice." She smoothed a hand over her hair. "I look awful."

"Not a chance. You look beautiful."

Nya frowned, doubtful. Then she asked, "What are you doing here?"

"There was a fire not too far from here. I wanted to swing by on the way back to the station, make sure you were okay. How're you feeling?"

A smile touched her lips. "I'm okay."

"How's your foot?"

"It still hurts a little."

"Have you been keeping it elevated?"

"I was." She gazed up at him and gave him a look of mock reproof. "Until you showed up, forcing me to get up from the sofa."

"My bad." He grinned down at her. Then he produced a couple of bags from just beyond Nya's view. They appeared to be filled with groceries. "This is for you."

"You went shopping for me?"

"Yeah, I picked you up some groceries. Before I left, I took the liberty of looking in your fridge and seeing what you didn't have. You had one egg left, barely any bread. No milk. I didn't know what you liked so I just picked up a bunch of stuff."

Nya's heart filled with happiness. He'd actually gone shopping for her? "Tyler, that's so sweet."

"It's no big deal. I want to make sure you have what you need so you don't have to run around on your injured foot."

Nya beamed at him. Had he really just done this? Or was she still dreaming?

And to think she had just been telling her support group how nice it was to have a man taking care of her.

This gesture had made her feel as special as his lips had the night before.

"You are too sweet, Tyler McKenzie."

"I aim to please."

Nya's gaze went to his lips. A special gesture deserved a special thank-you. She started to lean forward...

Tyler extended the bags to her. "Well, I'd better get out of here. The guys are waiting downstairs."

"Oh." Nya looked up at him in disappointment. He wasn't going to kiss her? "Of course." She swallowed. "Thank you so much for thinking of me."

"Text me if you need anything."

"Sure. Thanks again."

"Gotta go. I'll be in touch."

Tyler started down the stairs, and regret washed over Nya.

One good deed and she was weakening her resolve? She could just imagine what THEONLYWAY would say.

Of course, THEONLYWAY seemed to be totally opposed to dating at all. Her advice was never really tempered. Did the woman have no clue what it was like to be tempted?

Nya knew all about temptation and was glad that she was making strides and being strong. She was showing an element of restraint. Because honestly, with Tyler in her bed last night, she'd hoped that he would kiss her… even though she had also feared exactly that.

No, it's a good thing I didn't kiss Tyler, she decided.

Still, as Nya closed the door, she rested her back against it and sighed happily.

There was a part of her that wanted to call Sabrina and tell her what had just happened. How Tyler had bought her groceries, and how he'd been such a gentleman. How for the first time in a long time she was feeling a spark of interest in someone who seemed like a genuinely great guy.

Nya took the groceries to the kitchen then went back to the computer. She didn't want to go back to the chat and have THEONLYWAY put a pinprick into her balloon of happiness right now. Because there was something special about the fact that she and Tyler were clearly interested in each other, but that he wasn't pressuring her.

So Nya logged out of the chat room. And then she went back to the kitchen to fry some eggs, thinking about Tyler and smiling as she prepared her breakfast.

Chapter 11

Tyler was relaxing in the firehouse common room when Belinda, the administrative assistant, came in. "Tyler?" she said, approaching him.

"Hey, Belinda."

"Someone dropped by to see you when you guys were out at that fire."

Tyler's heart picked up speed. "Nya?"

Belinda handed him a sheet of paper. "It was a guy named John. He left a number for you to call him."

Tyler felt a sense of disappointment. He'd stopped by Nya's apartment on Saturday morning with groceries, and he'd hoped that she would have reached out to him after that. But she hadn't.

When he'd left her that morning, she had been smiling, and that had made him happy. After everything that had happened that night, Tyler had finally gotten a good sense of what was going on with Nya.

She said she wasn't hung up on Russell, and he believed her. But he also believed that Russell had left her scarred, and either she didn't trust men, or she didn't trust her own judgment where men were concerned anymore.

That was partly why Tyler hadn't kissed her on Saturday morning, even though he'd wanted to. He had been trying to show her that he was one of the good guys.

Tyler opened the folded sheet of paper. He hadn't heard from John Barker in over a year. John, who'd been Mr. Reliable, had broken up with his longtime girlfriend, Suzie, after meeting someone else, then had moved to Sacramento with her. After that, Tyler and John had fallen out of touch. Tyler suspected that it was because John had distanced himself from the friends he'd had when he and Suzie had been together, because many of them did not approve of how he'd broken Suzie's heart.

Still, Tyler missed their friendship, and so he dialed the number.

"Hey, John. It's Tyler."

"Tyler! Hey, man. I'm in town and wanted to reach out to you."

"I'm glad you did. Want to get together for a beer?" Tyler asked.

"Actually, remember Suzie?"

"Of course I remember her."

"Well, you're not going to believe it, but we're back together. In fact, we're getting married."

"What?"

"Yeah, I know. Even I didn't think it would happen. But that thing with Rita…it wasn't real. I'd been together with Suzie so long that I just started to doubt what we had. I guess…and I know this sounds awful…but I needed to know if there was something better out there."

"Yeah, relationships aren't easy," Tyler said.

"I'm just glad Suzie forgave me. I'm even moving back to town. And we're having an engagement party this weekend. I'm hoping you and Carol can make it."

Tyler swallowed. "Actually, Carol and I broke up."

"What? When?"

"About four months ago," Tyler explained. "I'm surprised Suzie didn't tell you."

"I never heard. Oh, man. I'm sorry."

"It wasn't meant to be," Tyler said, expressing a calmness he certainly hadn't felt at the time of his breakup. They'd been engaged when suddenly Carol had told him that she wasn't sure they had the kind of love that would last forever. She felt that they were making too serious a life decision too quickly. She wanted to spread her wings, find herself, and hoped that Tyler would understand and not hate her.

Carol had crushed his world, but Tyler was not about to hold her back. So he'd let her go.

"When's the party?" Tyler asked. "I'm off Saturday and Sunday."

"Saturday evening. It'll be a pool party. So bring your Speedo."

Tyler laughed. "Yeah, right. I can make it."

"But I imagine Carol will be there, too," John said, his voice taking on a more serious tone. "You still want to come?"

"I'll be there," Tyler said. "There's no doubt I'll see Carol at some point. May as well be at your party."

"All right. Good. I'm glad you'll be there. And no gifts, please. Suzie and I just want to reconnect and celebrate with our friends."

"Okay."

"It'll be at my parents' place. You remember where it is?"

"Of course." It was in an established, upper-middle-class neighborhood in the hills of Ocean City.

Suddenly, an idea came to Tyler. While he wasn't afraid to see Carol, he wasn't particularly keen on running into her. But if he had a date...

"Hey. Do you mind if I bring a friend?"

"Sure. Invite who you want." He paused. "Hey—is there someone new in your life?"

Was there someone new in his life? Would anything come of the sparks between him and Nya?

"A friend with potential," he told John.

"Great. Bring her. Can't wait to meet her."

As Tyler ended the call, he smiled. Nya was keeping her distance, and now Tyler had a reason for them to spend more time together. And he knew she couldn't refuse.

He had helped her out when she'd needed him to play her boyfriend. Now she could return the favor.

Nya's eyes widened and her lips parted when the front door of the studio opened and Tyler walked in. He was dressed in his casual firefighter attire—navy pants and a navy shirt with the Ocean City Fire Department logo emblazoned on the left side of the shirt.

He looked delectable. Good Lord, the way the form-fitting shirt hugged his muscular body, and the way those pants showcased his thighs… Nya had to swallow.

Rising, Nya said, "Hello, Tyler. Um, are you here to see Sabrina? She's out right now."

"Why would I be here to see Sabrina?"

"Um…about the calendar?" But even as Nya said that, she knew it sounded ridiculous.

He took a step forward and said, "I'm here to see you."

Nya swallowed again. "Oh."

"I'm at work," Tyler said. "I just popped over for a moment to ask you something."

"What do you want to ask me?"

Nya suddenly realized that her heart was beating at an extremely fast rate, and her skin felt flushed. Every time she saw Tyler, she got this reaction, and she wished she could turn it off.

She had spent the past few days telling herself that as long as he was out of sight, then she could keep him out of mind. But seeing him again proved that she had been lying to herself. She was secretly thrilled that he was here.

"I've got a proposition for you."

"Oh?"

"I have an engagement party to attend on Saturday. And my ex-fiancée will be there. I haven't seen her since we broke up, so I imagine it will be a little awkward. I'm kind of hoping that you can return the favor I did for you when I was your boyfriend." He made air quotes as he said the word *boyfriend*. "I'd love it if you'd go with me as my pretend girlfriend."

Disappointment squirmed in Nya's gut like a worm.

"Tyler…" Nya heaved a little sigh. "I'm not sure that's such a great idea. Me having you pretend to be my boyfriend was childish, and—"

"And yet we managed to have a good time."

Nya eyed him suspiciously. "Y-you had a good time?"

"Sure. Didn't you?"

"Even when I was weeping like an idiot?"

"Hey," Tyler said softly, moving closer to the reception desk. "You're not an idiot. You were upset. And yes, I had a good time with you. Even when I was wrapping your ankle."

Nya fought the urge to smile. Why did Tyler always know the perfect thing to say?

"About Friday night," Nya began softly. "I know you might be confused by my behavior. I guess I didn't properly explain where I'm at. But with all I've been through… I've been taking a break from dating. Trying to refocus on me."

There, she'd said it.

"I do understand," Tyler said. "And I think that you know by now that you can trust me not to take advantage of you."

He held her gaze. "Yes," she admitted. "I do know that."

But how could she tell him that he was dangerous to her plan, to her heart? The more time she spent with him, the more she didn't think she could resist him. And over these past few days, she had once again told herself that she *needed* to resist him, no matter how sweet nor how hot he was.

"I could really use someone there with me," Tyler went on, his voice light. "You know how unsettling it is to see your ex after you've both moved on. I just need you to be my date. It's a causal evening, no big flashy affair. And there'll be a ton of people there in case you get bored with me." He smiled. "Pool party. Barbecue. Come on, it'll be fun."

Nya wanted to say no. She really did. But she also knew just how selfish that would be. She had certainly used Tyler for the exact same purpose. How could she deny him?

"Saturday night?" she asked.

"Starts at five. Like I said, it's nothing big and fancy. It'll be a family barbecue with friends to celebrate my buddy's engagement. We don't even have to stay that long, if you don't want to."

"Okay. I'll go."

"Great. Can I pick you up at five?"

"I thought it started at five."

"Yeah, but we don't have to get there at the start. We can be fashionably late."

He grinned, and it was all but impossible to deny him when he smiled at her like that. "Sure," Nya said. "Five o'clock will be fine."

"All right." He held her gaze for a beat. "How's your ankle, by the way?"

"Feeling a lot better. I've gotten used to rewrapping it after every shower. You still did a better job, but it's been okay."

"You should have called me. I would have helped out."

Nya got the sense that he wasn't speaking in jest. That if she'd needed him, he would have been there for her. "Duly noted," Nya said.

A few beats passed, and Nya stared at Tyler, wondering if he was going to kiss her.

"Look," he began, "I've got to get back to the station. I'll be in touch before Saturday."

Nya nodded. "Okay."

As Tyler left, she found herself frowning. Once again, he hadn't tried to kiss her. Even though she'd told him that Sabrina wasn't there.

Good Lord, what was wrong with her? What would the members of her support group say if they knew she were wishing for a kiss from Tyler?

One minute, she was telling him that she was taking a break from dating. The next, she was upset that he'd walked away without giving her a kiss.

She couldn't have it both ways.

The phone rang at the same time that the door chimes sang. Nya reached for the receiver, but her hand stilled when she saw Tyler walk back in through the door.

Her nerves began to do a happy dance in her stomach. "Did you forget something?"

"Yes," Tyler said.

He stalked toward her, and Nya drew in a sharp breath. What was he doing?

In the next instant, Tyler rounded the desk and swept her into his arms. His strong body pressed against hers, and he flattened a hand on her back to keep her close. Then he whispered in her ear, "This is what I forgot."

His lips came down on hers. The heat was instant, the explosion of sensations delicious.

God, how Nya had wanted to do this again. Have another taste of him. The passion between them was undeniable.

Just as she snaked her arms around his neck and fully surrendered to the kiss, he eased back. "I get that you've been hurt," Tyler said, his voice raspy. "So I know you want to be cautious. But I don't want there to be any confusion. I like you, Nya. *A lot.*"

Then he released her and left, leaving Nya breathing raggedly and wanting more.

So much more.

Chapter 12

All Tuesday night, Nya was a hot mess.

A hot and bothered mess.

I don't want there to be any confusion. I like you, Nya. A lot.

She'd dreamed about having sex with him. Scorching, toe-tingling sex.

What killed her was the fact that there'd been no text from him. No call. He'd kissed her, and left her wanting more…and he hadn't even sent a message to let her know that he was thinking of her.

Was he thinking about her? Or had he been able to kiss her and go on about his day?

I like you, Nya. A lot.

Nya liked him, too. And her resolve to push him away had all but disappeared. He'd occupied her thoughts all of Tuesday night, and she'd woken Wednesday morning hoping more than anything that she would hear from him today.

It was her birthday. And today of all days, she wanted to know that he was thinking of her.

Of course, she hadn't told him that it was her birthday, so he couldn't know. But a call just because, or even a text would brighten her mood.

Especially since Sabrina had forgotten her birthday.

She'd left first thing in the morning for a conference booking, and Nya knew that she was busy. But still…it stung a little that her friend hadn't remembered that Nya turned thirty-four today.

Nya woke her phone from sleep mode and pulled up the photo of Tyler she'd saved.

She all but salivated every time she looked at the picture. After that kiss yesterday, she thought for sure that she would hear from him.

And today of all days, it mattered.

Why don't you just text him? Tell him it's your birthday?

But even as the idea came to Nya, she dismissed it. She wanted him to reach out to her because he missed her, not because he felt some sense of obligation.

At three o'clock, Nya's phone trilled with a text message. She quickly grabbed her phone and checked her messages. It was from a friend, wishing her a happy birthday.

Nya frowned. Had Tyler forgotten her?

The very idea had Nya's stomach twisting, but then she remembered what Mason had said. That Tyler was one of the good guys.

She also remembered Tyler's own words. *I get that you've been hurt. So I know you want to be cautious.*

Was that why he was giving her space? Any other guy would have already followed up and tried to take her to bed.

Clearly, Tyler wasn't like other men.

Nya didn't *want* to want him, but there was no denying the truth. Maybe if it weren't her birthday, she could try to push her desires aside and remember her vow to abstain from dating. But no girl wanted to be alone on her birthday.

Just before four o'clock, Sabrina breezed into the studio, harried and out of breath. She off-loaded her heavy camera bag onto the floor then pushed her sunglasses into her hair. "Oh, my goodness. That was a crazy day."

Nya got to her feet. "Let me help you." She rounded the desk and took the smaller camera bag and tripod from Sabrina. "You look exhausted."

"I am. I didn't know a corporate event could be so taxing. You know, I think I ought to train you to take photos so you can help me out."

Nya's stomach fluttered. "Seriously?"

Sabrina walked over to the water cooler and began to pour water into a cone cup. "Why not? I think you've got the aptitude."

Nya narrowed her eyes. Where was this coming from? Tyler hadn't said something to Mason about her interest in photography, had he? "I'd never be as good as you."

Sabrina drank her water then said, "Never say never."

Nya gave her an update on the new consultations from the day. "I *am* going to have to get you working with me," Sabrina said. "I can't keep up with all this work."

"Speaking of which, that guy Darryl called back again. Reiterated that he'd love to work with you if you need another photographer."

Sabrina's lips twisted slightly. "I might have to consider it. But for now, I'm managing." Exhaling loudly, Sabrina plopped onto the leather arm chair she had in the waiting room. "I can't wait to go home and take a hot bath with epsom salts."

"Nothing special planned for the evening?" Nya asked.

"No, nothing special," Sabrina said. "I'll probably go to dinner with Mason if he wants. Or we'll just stay in."

Nya forced a smile. Heck, she wished that Sabrina

had a full evening of events planned. At least then she would feel better about Sabrina forgetting her birthday.

"Sweetie, will you do me a favor?" Sabrina asked. "I'm so tired. Will you take my camera bag and tripod back to the studio for me? You know where the stuff goes."

Nya nodded. "Sure."

She gathered up the gear and brought it back to the studio to put away.

"You want me to bring your smaller camera bag back, too?" Nya was asking as she made her way back into the reception area. She stopped in her tracks when she saw the smiling faces of Sabrina, Mason and Tyler. Tyler was holding a cake lit up with a blinding number of candles, while Sabrina was holding a camera.

Nya stopped, stunned.

"Happy birthday to you, happy birthday to you, happy birthday, dear Nya, happy birthday to you!" they all sang, laughing at her expression.

When they were finished, Nya put her hands over her mouth and giggled. Then she said, "How many candles is that? I'm only thirty-four."

Sabrina snapped a photo of her then said, "Get over here."

As Tyler put the cake onto the counter, Sabrina hugged her. Then Mason hugged her and wished her a happy birthday. Finally, Tyler enveloped her in his strong embrace and kissed her temple. "Happy birthday, gorgeous."

Nya shot a glance at Sabrina and Mason, who were staring at her with knowing eyes. Then Sabrina snapped another photo.

"Thank you," Nya said softly. Then, facing Sabrina, she said, "I thought you forgot."

Sabrina laughed. "I know. The look on your face when I told you I was doing nothing tonight…it was priceless."

"You got me," Nya admitted.

"Why didn't you tell me it was your birthday?" Tyler asked her.

"I…I don't know."

She noticed then that Mason and Tyler were dressed in nice slacks and shirts. "Why are you dressed up?"

"Because we have dinner reservations," Sabrina said, smiling proudly. "We're going to celebrate your birthday with you."

"But I'm not dressed up," Nya protested. She looked down at her denim skirt and simple blouse.

"You always look amazing," Tyler said.

Nya's stomach fluttered. It wasn't just the words; it was the way he was looking at her. Lord, how she wanted him…

"Where are we going?" Nya asked.

"You love that Mexican-American fusion place," Sabrina began, "so that's where we're going." She turned to Mason. "You ready, babe?"

Mason put his arm around her waist. "Yep."

As they headed to the door, Sabrina threw a glance over her shoulder. "By the way, we're gonna take separate cars."

Then she winked.

Nya's breath caught in her throat. Were Sabrina and Mason playing matchmaker?

Tyler placed a gentle hand on her back. "After you."

"Let me just get my purse."

"Well, here we are," Tyler announced three and a half hours later when he pulled up in front of Nya's house.

Looking at him, Nya giggled. "Yep. This is my house."

Tyler hid his smirk. She'd had three margaritas—one too many. She'd been extra happy ever since the third one had kicked in.

"Hold on," Tyler said, then exited the vehicle. He walked around to the passenger-side door and opened it for her.

Even though Nya took his hand, she still clumsily got out, faltering and falling against him. "Oops."

"You all right?" Tyler asked, helping her steady herself.

"I'm great."

Tyler started walking with her to the door. He took the steps slowly with her. She still had her ankle wrapped, but it was more her inebriated state that he was concerned about now.

"Thank you," she said when they were at her door. Her grin was extra wide. "I had a good time."

"So did I," Tyler said. He'd enjoyed seeing Nya laugh and smile. They'd insisted on embarrassing her by having the restaurant staff sing her happy birthday, while making her stand and wear a wackily decorated sombrero on her head. Sabrina, of course, had taken several photos.

As Nya gazed up at him, her smile slowly disappeared, while her eyes widened. Tyler felt a pull in his groin, knowing that she was waiting for a kiss.

But he also knew that she was a little tipsy. And he didn't want to take advantage of her when she didn't have all of her wits about her.

Stuffing his hands into his pockets, Tyler asked, "You've got your key?"

Nya dug into her purse until she found it. She raised it high. "Got it."

"Good. Open the door."

She made no move to turn from him. Instead, she pouted. "You don't like me, do you?"

Tyler's eyes bulged. "Don't like you?"

"You don't even want to kiss me."

"Of course I want to kiss you," he said. "But I'm trying to be a gentleman."

She stepped closer to him and slipped her arms around his waist. "You didn't want to kiss me Saturday morning. And you left yesterday without kissing me."

"Have you forgotten that I returned to kiss you?" he asked.

"No," she said, her voice wispy. "That's what's had me wrecked since last night."

Tyler chuckled. "Wrecked? Gee, I don't think anyone has ever said that my kiss left them *wrecked* before."

"In a good way," Nya added in a silky whisper as she wrapped her arms around his neck and pressed her breasts against his body.

"Damn it, Nya. I'm trying—"

"You're not trying hard enough," she said. Then she eased up on her toes and kissed him.

Tyler wanted to pull her away from him. Be a total gentleman and resist her. But oh, man. With her lips on his, and her fingers trilling the back of his neck, and those sweet little sighs coming from her lips, Tyler was losing his resolve.

"Nya," he managed. "You should go upstairs. I'll see you Saturday night."

She tightened her arms around him. "No. Don't leave me."

She reconnected the kiss. Her mouth moved over his with more urgency, and her tongue flicked against his lips, seeking entry. Growling out a groan, he opened his mouth, and her warm, sweet tongue slipped between his lips.

Nya purred and ran a finger down his back. Despite Tyler's best efforts, his member hardened.

But still he managed to tear his lips from hers. "Nya…"

"I know. I should open the door." She chuckled softly. "We don't want to get arrested for having sex on my doorstep."

Sex on my doorstep… The words made his arousal throb. "Nya, sweetheart. You've had too much to drink."

She eased back and looked at him, and he could see the hint of disappointment in her eyes. "You think I don't know what I'm doing?"

"I…" Tyler forced out a breath. He wished his body would cooperate and not get aroused. But damn it, Nya was gorgeous, and she was sweet, and she was utterly tempting. "The last thing I want to do is take advantage of you."

"I want you," she whispered. "I knew that before I ever had a sip of alcohol."

Tyler swallowed. And then Nya was running her fingers over his chest and kissing his jaw. A groan rumbling in his chest, Tyler forced her body backward so that she was against the railing. And God help him, he was powerless as she touched him.

Gently slipping his hands into her hair, he planted his lips on hers and kissed her as if his very existence depended on it.

"Yes," Nya said on a breathy sigh. And Tyler knew that if they made it upstairs, there would be no turning back. He hadn't felt an all-consuming passion like this in…

Had he ever felt an attraction this powerful? Even with Carol, their sexual chemistry had never been this fierce.

Someone driving by hit the horn and startled them.

Both he and Nya looked toward the street then began to chuckle.

"I think we're risking arrest for public indecency," Tyler said, cradling her in his arms.

"Oh, heck!" Nya suddenly said.

Tyler looked at her with concern. "What?"

"I'm supposed to go to my parents'." She closed her eyes and groaned.

Tyler's aroused body felt as though it had suddenly been doused in cold water. "R-right now?"

"I'm so sorry. My parents are heading out of town in the morning for my aunt's retirement party. I can't make it, but I have to sign the card we're giving her, as well as drop off my gift—which is in my purse. Will you take me there?"

"You want me to meet your parents?"

"Well, that would be a bit awkward," she conceded. "But if you drop me off…then you can pick me up." Her voice rose on a hopeful note.

Tyler forced in a slow, calming breath. As disappointed as he was, he also knew that this was best. When she was finished visiting her parents, her mind would be clear of any effect of alcohol. And if she still wanted him then…

Then there would be no doubts.

All through her visit with her parents, Nya was giddy. And it had nothing to do with the alcohol she'd consumed earlier.

Yes, she was intoxicated. But she was intoxicated with Tyler McKenzie.

There was no doubt that the margaritas had given her some liquid courage to go for what she wanted. And for her birthday, she wanted Tyler.

The passion between them was off the charts. She'd

had to try to keep the smile off her face while she'd thought of him almost every second. Everything about him made her smile. He was a gentleman, he was seriously sexy, and their bodies spoke to each other with some major heat.

At least today, on her birthday, she didn't want to deny herself. That wasn't wrong, was it?

When Tyler picked her up just after nine, and she saw the way his face lit up when he saw her, she had her answer.

No. It wasn't wrong. In fact, she couldn't remember anything ever feeling this right.

"Did you have a good visit?" Tyler asked once she was in the car beside him.

"It was nice. They spoiled me with a gift card to my favorite store. I love them."

"Sounds like you have a good relationship with them."

"Are you not on good terms with your parents?"

"My parents split when I was fifteen," he said. "My dad lives in Oklahoma with his new wife. But my mom… she passed a couple of years ago. Breast cancer."

"Oh, Tyler." Nya reached for his hand and squeezed it. "I'm so sorry. I can't even imagine losing one of my parents."

"It's awful," Tyler told her. "Especially when you're close. And my mother…she was my everything."

Nya didn't think. She just stroked his face in a comforting gesture. Tyler turned his lips into her palm and kissed it.

"Tell me about her," Nya said.

"She was beautiful," Tyler said. "And I don't just mean on the outside. She was one of the sweetest people anyone could ever meet. She taught special-needs kids all of her life, and I can't tell you how many of them were at the funeral."

"That must have made you feel proud."

"It did." Tyler paused, and a smile touched his lips. "She was also funny. She was known for her practical jokes." He chuckled softly at the memory of something. "Yeah, she was a great mom."

"I'm sorry you lost her," Nya said.

Tyler faced her briefly. "I ran the 10K run for the cure last month in her honor. I raised a couple of grand."

"That's wonderful. I'm sure she's looking down on you with pride."

"Thanks," Tyler said.

They drove the next few minutes to her house in silence, and Nya wondered why a man like Tyler hadn't been snatched up by someone already. He truly seemed like one of the good ones. A genuinely nice guy.

He pulled up in front of her house. "Here we—"

Nya leaned across the front seat and silenced him with a kiss. Then she whispered, "My head is totally clear. Come up with me."

Tyler cleared his throat. "Let me, um, park the car."

Biting on her bottom lip, Nya exited the vehicle. Heat pulsing through her veins, she watched him drive down the street and park on the other side.

No human should be that sexy, she thought. He was wearing different clothes, jeans and a T-shirt now, and smelled of aftershave. Nya figured he had showered while she was with her parents.

He grinned as he stepped in front of her, and her body tightened with sexual anticipation. She had to kiss him.

So she planted her hands on his chest and eased upward. He lowered his mouth to meet hers, and though the kiss was sweet and tender, Nya felt sparks.

"Let's not risk getting arrested," Tyler whispered.

Nya giggled. Then she made her way up the steps.

As she slipped the key into the lock, Tyler placed his hands on her hips. Heat flooded her.

Nya quickly unlocked the door and pushed it open. She stepped inside, and Tyler followed her.

Nya began to climb the stairs to her floor in front of Tyler, figuring that his eyes were checking out her bottom as she moved. She wished she were wearing something sexier. Although what she was wearing would not matter for long…

A fire was brewing within her, and she was glad that a fireman was here to put it out. Because that was exactly what she needed.

Maybe she was crazy. Because she had gone from one extreme to the other. Telling herself that she needed to abstain, but now wanting nothing more than to make love to this gorgeous man.

She got to the top level. By the time she started unlocking the door, Tyler's hands were smoothing over her hips and her behind.

She dropped her head against his shoulder. "Tyler, you're distracting me."

He bent his head to kiss her lips. "I can't help myself."

A heavenly sigh escaped her. Briefly, she thought of the online support group. Imagined that THEONLYWAY would be livid if she knew what Nya was about to do.

But no one else was in her shoes. How did you resist someone who was irresistible?

Raising her head, Nya unlocked the door and stepped into her unit. As she flicked on the light, her eyes swept over the disarray. The papers on the coffee table. The vacuum cleaner in the corner of the living room. The basket of laundry by the sofa.

"I'm sorry," she said, turning to face him. "The place is a—"

He pulled her into his arms. "All I see is you."

Nya's body pulsed. "You always know the right thing to say."

Tyler put his lips to her ear and whispered, "I have something for you."

"Mmm," Nya moaned, figuring he was speaking about what he would *give* her in the bedroom. Then she began to kiss the underside of his jaw.

"Wait," Tyler said, and eased away from her.

Nya looked up at him, confused.

"I have this." He dug into the back pocket of his jeans. "Guess I could have put it in a box, but when I found out it was your birthday, I didn't have much time."

"You got me something for my birthday?" Nya asked.

"I didn't know what you wanted, but I figured you could use this."

Tyler handed her a small envelope. As she accepted it, Nya recognized the name of a local camera shop. "Tyler, you—you didn't have to."

"I *wanted* to," he said. "It's a gift card," he added, just as Nya noticed the dollar amount written on the front of the envelope.

"It's too much," Nya told him.

"It's enough to pay for a photography course. I didn't know which one you'd be interested in, so you can decide for yourself. Or you can use it to buy some supplies. Whatever you want."

She had barely talked to him about her interest in photography, and he had already bought her something to support that interest? Nya looked up at him. "B-but why?"

He encircled her waist with his arms and whispered, "Because I like you."

His words touched her deep in the core of her being. He was the most thoughtful, kind and gorgeous man she had ever met. Was he too good to be true?

Right now, she didn't care.

Chapter 13

Nya pressed her body against Tyler's and snaked her arms around his neck. "I like you, too."

With a growl of lust, Tyler brought his head down and kissed her. And as his lips played over hers, he slipped a hand underneath her shirt. Her entire body became flushed as his warm palm covered the small of her back.

Every single time he touched her, it was explosive. Nya was hot and bothered and wanted Tyler like she'd wanted no one before.

She tightened her arms around his neck. Standing right there in her entranceway, they kissed like teenagers in heat.

"You are so sexy," Tyler said. "Do you know that?"

His words were like an aphrodisiac, making her light-headed with desire. Oh, she had missed this. Missed the rush of emotion, the rush of lust from a man's touch.

And not just any man. A sexy one.

And one who liked you back.

But as much as she liked him, she didn't want to feel any pressure to jump into a relationship. So in the back of her mind, she told herself to take this night for what it was. An opportunity to satisfy a sexual need.

She was making an exception to her no-dating hiatus only because it was her birthday.

Nya pushed his shirt upward, exposing his chest. It was smooth and rippled with muscles. Tearing her lips from his, she lowered her mouth to his torso and kissed him there. He groaned, so she kissed him again and again, moving lower and lower each time. His purely masculine smell was driving her mad with lust. He was wearing a musky cologne that made him even more tantalizing.

Tyler pulled his shirt over his head, and Nya took a moment to stare at his beautiful form. She remembered his large biceps and chiseled abs from the calendar. But in real life, he was even hotter.

"You say I'm sexy, but damn, Tyler." She stroked his stomach. "You are seriously hot."

Tyler pulled her into his arms and once again planted his lips on hers. He began to move toward the bedroom, forcing her to walk backward as his mouth and tongue played over hers.

His hands were underneath her shirt, his palms running all over her body. Outside her bedroom door, he paused. "I'm glad you're not wearing that dress you had on Friday night."

Nya looked up at him. "You didn't like the dress?"

"I loved it. But I knew it wouldn't be easy to get off you." He pecked her lips again. "This, however…" He gripped the bottom edge of her shirt in his hands then pulled the shirt off her. "Yes," he said, his eyes settling on her body. "I don't have to fight this outfit to get to what I want." He blew out a low whistle. "Damn, Nya… you're perfect."

Nya had never felt more beautiful. She saw lust in Tyler's gaze and knew that their sexual chemistry was off the charts. But she also saw something else in his gaze. Something that made her feel like this wasn't just sex.

Nya squealed as Tyler swept her into his arms. Then he carried her across the threshold to the bedroom. As he did, Nya rested her head in the crook of his neck. How sexy was this? A man carrying her to her bedroom? It was a simple thing, and yet it gave her a sexual charge.

The lights in the room were off, but the blinds were open, allowing the lights from the street to softly illuminate the room. It was just enough light to see what they were doing, and enough darkness to add to the sense of intimacy.

His lips finding hers again, he carried her until they reached the bed. Then he lowered her and said, "Turn around."

Nya's heart was beating out of control as she turned over. He swept her hair over one shoulder and kissed the back of her neck and then her shoulder blade. A shiver of desire danced down Nya's spine.

His hands went to the back of her denim skirt, and he began to unbutton it, all the while brushing kisses along her upper back. He helped her shimmy her skirt past her hips. She heard his exhalation of breath when he saw her bottom—mostly exposed in her thong underwear.

His hands went to the back of her bra. Within a few moments, he had it unclasped. Gently kissing the back of her neck again, he slipped the straps down her arms until her body was free of her bra.

Slowly, he turned her. His eyes met hers and held them. He stroked her cheek before his gaze went lower, finally taking in the sight of her naked breasts.

"Baby," he said softly. "You're the most beautiful woman I've ever seen."

Nya believed him. And when Tyler gently ran his fingers down the length of her left arm before taking her hand in his, she felt beautiful. Desired. And respected.

This was a man who knew not to rush. A man who knew how to play out every moment of passion.

"Take off your panties for me," he whispered.

Releasing his hand, Nya drew in a deep breath. After this, there was no turning back. Did she want this?

Oh, yes. She'd never felt so sure of something in her life.

She shimmied the panties down her legs, feeling the heat of his gaze as she did. Once they were off, she stood. He met her eyes and held her gaze. Held her gaze even as he placed his palm gently on her cheek. Nya curled into his palm, and her eyes fluttered shut.

"Look at me."

Nya opened her eyes, saw Tyler's heated gaze once more.

"I want you to see me seeing you. Seeing how much I want you."

So she watched him. Watched as he fully checked out her nude body. Had she ever done exactly this before? Watched the way a man's eyes changed as he regarded her? His desire for her was a palpable thing. She saw it in the way his chest rose, the way his eyes darkened as he drank in the sight of her.

It was erotic.

Heat struck her feminine core. His eyes had been like a torch, leaving warmth wherever they had touched her.

Tyler's hands followed the path his eyes had taken. They moved over her cheek then down her neck and then over her breast. His fingers closed around one nipple, and he tweaked until it hardened beneath his touch. "I want to take my time with you. But I don't know if I can."

A soft moan escaped Nya's lips. The way he was looking at her gave her a charge she'd never experienced before.

He stepped toward her again, closing the distance between them. His hands went to both of her breasts while his mouth found hers. He kissed her, his tongue sweeping through her mouth with wide, hot strokes. It was intoxicating.

And then he lowered his mouth to her breast. He flicked his tongue over her nipple, and Nya cried out from the delicious sensation.

Then he drew her nipple into his mouth and began to suckle.

The sensations that flooded her body were pure bliss.

Tyler moved his mouth to her other breast, and he sucked that nipple with an increased sense of urgency. As he did, he placed his hands on her back and moved her to the bed. Nya's knees buckled when they hit the mattress, and she sat.

Stepping backward, Tyler undid his jeans and slipped them off.

A breath oozed out of her. *Oh, dear God.* She'd seen just how stunning he had looked with his shirt off, but she wasn't prepared for how delectable he looked without a stitch of clothing on. His arousal was large and impressive. His naked body was absolute perfection.

She couldn't believe that he was about to make love to her.

Tyler approached her. He bent his body over hers so that she could remain sitting on the edge of the bed. Framing her face with his hand, he angled her head up to his while lowering his mouth to meet hers.

And when their lips connected, it was as if she had been touched by a live wire. Her entire body was electrified.

As his tongue tangled with hers, Tyler urged her body backward. Within seconds, she was lying on her back, and he was easing his body beside hers. He nibbled her bottom lip while placing his hand over her breast. He played with her nipple, and Nya moaned.

"Yes, baby," Tyler rasped. And then he lowered his head to her breast and began to suckle her nipple again.

Nya arched her back, her body throbbing. And then Tyler was smoothing a hand down her torso. He found the center of her womanhood and gently stroked her there.

"You're ready for me," he said, looking into her eyes.

His mouth was hovered above her breast, and his hand was between her thighs. Nya could explode from the electric sensations at any moment.

"I've been ready for a long time," she admitted softly. And she had been. From the moment she'd kissed him, she had envisioned what it would be like to make love to him.

His tongue tantalized her nipple again while his fingers almost sent her over the edge. She felt excitement and desire so intense, it was as if a man were touching her for the first time.

She stretched a foot over his body and stroked his upper back. "Make love to me," she pleaded.

Tyler brought his lips to hers again and gave her a languid, delicious kiss before easing off the bed. Nya was breathless as she looked at him. She watched him go to his jeans and withdraw a condom from the back pocket. Watched as he put it onto his member.

She drew in a sharp breath when he started toward her with determination. He knelt onto the bed, and she moved backward to give him room. And then he was touching her face and kissing her, his warm tongue sweeping the interior of her mouth with broad, desperate strokes. And as he touched her and kissed her, he settled himself between her thighs.

"Baby," Nya said. Her voice was faint and filled with longing. She pressed her palms flat against his back as she spread her legs wider.

Tyler moved his mouth to her ear and nibbled on her sensitive flesh. But nothing compared to the pleasure that flooded her as Tyler guided himself inside her.

Nya gripped his shoulders. "Oh, Tyler!"

"Nya," he responded, his voice gruff. "Sweetheart…"

He eased inside her slowly, drawing out her pleasure. He filled her completely, made her whole body come alive.

"Tyler," she murmured. "Oh, my goodness."

Slowly, he began to move in and out. Nya dug her fingers into his back and pressed her lips against his shoulder as each stroke brought her bliss.

"Look at me, baby," Tyler said.

Nya raised her eyes and looked at him. Looked at him as their bodies found a rhythm. As they found a rhythm that was their own.

Had Nya ever felt this connected to another human being? Had anything ever felt this good?

He thrust deep into her, and Nya gasped. Tyler kissed her, swallowing her fervent cries.

Locking her legs around him, she held on for the passionate ride. And as their pace quickened and their kiss deepened, Nya felt her body reaching the edge.

Tyler kissed a path to her ear and suckled her earlobe. And that's what did it. Pushed her over the edge into an abyss of glorious sensations.

"Tyler…" she cried, gripping him so hard she might break his skin. "Oh, my God."

"I'm here, baby," he whispered into her ear.

His own moans deepened, and his pace became quicker still. And soon, he was joining her in the abyss.

He kissed her again. Kissed her until they both collapsed into each other's arms.

"Happy birthday," he said, looking down at her.

Nya laughed and tightened her legs and arms around him. "My birthday's not over yet."

"Don't you worry," he whispered. "I'm not through with you yet. Not by a long shot."

Chapter 14

Nya was on cloud nine after her night with Tyler. Oh, man. What a night it had been. His skills between the sheets had been unbelievable, and Nya had had the best birthday *ever*.

"What are you so happy about?" Sabrina asked her as she walked into work. Suddenly, Sabrina gasped, and her eyes bulged. "Oh, my goodness! You and Tyler... So you two hit it off?"

"He's a sweetheart," Nya responded, and sighed dreamily. "And a stallion. We had a great time."

"Woo hoo!"

Nya eyed her suspiciously. "Why are you so happy? What happened to the Sabrina who agreed that I should take a break from dating?"

"Not *forever*," Sabrina said. "And Mason says that Tyler is a great guy. He's not a player. He was seriously involved with someone until about four months ago."

"His ex-fiancée," Nya said. That was the one thing that gave her pause, especially with the barbecue on Saturday. Had he really moved on after her? Or was he too good to be true?

Late Saturday afternoon, Tyler pulled up in front of Nya's house and saw her standing on the front step. He blew out a low whistle. He'd told her this wasn't a dress-up event, and granted, she wasn't in a ball gown. But she was wearing a multicolored sundress and strappy gold sandals, and she looked stunning. No matter what she wore, she looked amazing.

No matter what she wore... Tyler remembered all too well just how good she'd looked out of clothes.

He felt a jolt in his groin and knew he needed to think of something nonsexual before he embarrassed himself.

"Cute baby bunnies," he muttered to himself as he opened the door and got out of the Lincoln. He smiled and walked toward Nya, who was already at the car's passenger door.

"Hello, Nya." He wrapped his arms around her and had to swallow when her beautiful, feminine body pressed against his. He stepped backward. "You have your swimming stuff in that bag?"

"Yes," she said. "Although I don't know if I'll go into the pool. I've been wanting to get to the gym to tone up."

Tyler's eyes widened as he took the bag from her. "What are you talking about? You have an amazing body."

"I've lost a little weight. But I feel I could do some toning up."

"Nonsense," Tyler said. He put the bag in the backseat of the car then moved over to her. "You're beautiful." He couldn't help himself and began stroking her face. "And your body..."

He drew in a sharp breath and took a step backward. They'd be even more late to the party if this continued. Because talking about her body had him remembering her naked in his arms...and heat was now coursing through his veins.

"Thank you." Nya gave him a bashful look then glanced away.

Tyler opened the car door for her. She got in, and he tried not to check out her shapely hips, nor that expanse of brown leg. Nor those sandals, which were seriously sexy.

Cute baby bunnies, he told himself as he walked back to the driver's side of the car.

"Oh, wait," he said before he started the car. "Do you have your camera?"

Nya shook her head. "Just my phone."

"Why don't you get your camera? I was thinking you could take some pictures of the event."

Nya's eyes flew to his. "What?"

"Capture his engagement party. If you get some great shots, I can compile them in an album for John and Suzie as an engagement present."

Nya stared at him, her eyes filled with confusion. "Tyler, I told you I'm not really pursuing photography."

"That's why you have that expensive camera?"

"Well, I don't fancy myself a photographer. I'm just a hobbyist. I hardly know what I'm doing."

"Don't put yourself down," he said. "Get your camera. Take a few pictures. If they're not great, you don't have to do anything with them."

Nya opened her mouth, and Tyler thought she was about to protest. But instead she said, "All right. I'll be right back."

He watched her disappear out of the car. A couple minutes later, she was back with a camera bag.

"Have you told Sabrina?" Tyler asked when she got into the car beside him.

Nya's eyes bulged. "That I want to take pictures? No, of course not."

"Why not?"

"Because…I don't want her thinking that I'm crazy."

"Why would she think you're crazy? I thought you guys were good friends."

"We're best friends. I guess…I just don't want to embarrass myself. You know—photography is something I'm developing a passion for, but I'm hardly good at it."

Tyler didn't know if the people in her life had always discouraged her rather than supported her, but Nya was clearly uncomfortable going after what she wanted. "Hey," he said gently, as he started the car, "if you like it, pursue it. Don't let anyone hold you back."

Nya offered him a small smile. "I appreciate that, but like I said, I'm just playing around. I'm a hobbyist, just as many people are. I like pictures. That's all."

"You sound as though people have always questioned your dreams and not supported you."

Her lips parted in surprise, and she gave him an odd look. It was a look that told him she was stunned he had figured that out.

"I'll take pictures," Nya said. "Hopefully, some of them will be good."

Tyler started to drive. "The house is about a twenty-minute drive up into the hills. It's a lovely place. My buddy's parents have an awesome view of the ocean and the valley. It's a great spot for parties."

Nya nodded. "I'm looking forward to it."

Tyler was unsure of what to say. They'd had a great night together, and now this was supposed to be a pretend date. Of course, Wednesday had taken the notion of *pretend* off the table.

But still, it wasn't like they'd defined their relationship. He knew she'd talked about taking a break from dating, but would she reconsider that? Or had Wednesday night simply been about a hookup?

He didn't want to scare her off by pushing too hard, too fast. He was prepared to take things slowly for as long as she needed.

Which was hard, given that even now, she had him thinking about getting naked.

Tyler played an old-school CD mix, and as he began to drive, they were both quiet, just listening to the music. He glanced at Nya often, saw that she was either gazing out the window or looking down at her hands. Clearly, she was feeling the same post-sex awkwardness that he was. Unless she felt he'd been pushing her too much about her photography.

"I see you're not wearing the wrap on your ankle anymore," Tyler said.

"Yeah. It feels fine now."

"I'm glad."

"You know," Nya began softly, "what you said about people not supporting me… I guess you're right."

Tyler glanced at her, surprised that she was opening up. "Go on."

"I come from a family that believes in tangible careers. Like teaching or law or the medical field. Years ago, I wanted to go into fashion design, but they never understood that. And they told me the idea was ridiculous."

"Do you make your own clothes?" Tyler asked, his eyes taking in her outfit once more.

"No. But I do care a lot about good fashion." She paused then continued. "I always knew I wanted to do something creative. That's just who I was. But no one supported me. I have an older brother who was the brainy child. He went into medicine, and now he's got some big position in a New York hospital. I guess compared to him, I'm a disappointment to my family."

"Hey," Tyler said softly. She was looking at her hands again. "Look at me," he urged.

She did, and he could see the disappointment in her eyes. The years of crushed dreams.

"You get one life," he said. "You have to do what you want. Not what your parents want. That'll lead to resentment. And years of unhappiness."

Nya sighed softly. "I did end up working for a doctor's office as a secretary. I made a decent income, but you're right—I hated every moment of it. I guess that's partly why when I met Russell, I was so excited. He was working on a feature, and I started helping him out, and I was enjoying that spark that came from doing something creative. I was already working for Sabrina at the time, which I was loving, too. But she had her creative outlet in photography. I craved that, and thought I'd found it with Russell's project. But you know how that turned out."

Was that part of why she'd been so upset by her breakup with Russell? Because she'd lost part of her career dream, as well?

"If film is what you want to do—"

"Actually, I think I just fell in love with the idea of film because I was with Russell." She paused. "But when I started working with Sabrina, I fell in love with photography. I just didn't think I could do it. After things fell apart with Russell, I got a camera, started taking pictures. I guess that somewhere in the back of my mind I hope that Sabrina and I can one day be partners. I know that sounds silly."

"It doesn't sound silly," Tyler told her. "It sounds like you've found a new passion that can be totally fulfilling for you."

Her eyes lit up with a smile. She didn't have to say it, but he knew that his words had meant a lot to her.

"What about you?" she asked. "Was firefighting what you always wanted to do?"

"Always," Tyler said. "Actually, I think I wanted to be an astronaut at one point. Then a veterinarian. And there was definitely a time when I wanted to be a school bus driver. I saw that big yellow bus and thought it would be cool to drive it around."

Nya chuckled. "What—when you were four?"

"Pretty much," Tyler said, and laughed with her. But he quickly became serious. "And then I turned nine. And my best friend died in a house fire."

The humor dissipated from Nya's face. "Oh, Tyler. I'm so sorry."

"It was a long time ago. Twenty-six years."

"But it still hurts," Nya said. "I can see that."

Tyler nodded slowly. "Even now, I don't understand. Someone was cooking in the middle of the night, and the fire started in the townhouse beside theirs. LaShaw— that was his name—was trapped in his bedroom. His mother was able to get his little sister out but not him." Tyler paused, swallowed. "I still remember the moment I heard about the fire. LaShaw was supposed to sleep over at my house the next day. I kept thinking that if only he had slept over that night, he wouldn't be dead. In my nine-year-old mind, I blamed myself."

Nya reached for his hand. "Tyler, that's heartbreaking."

"We'd been best friends since kindergarten. And when I lost him, I also remember thinking that if only firefighters had gotten there sooner, they could have saved him. So at nine years old, I vowed to become a firefighter so that I could save people."

"You're really incredible," Nya said softly. "To have

that sort of resolve at that young age. To vow to do something to help, instead of feeling helpless…"

Tyler squeezed her hand. "I just knew that I never wanted to feel that way again. I had my mother take me to the firehouse near us, and the guys there got to know me. They let me climb into the trucks and try on the helmets and boots. My love for firefighting grew, and the moment I was old enough, I pursued it. Haven't looked back."

He glanced at Nya, and she was smiling at him. It felt as though they'd just passed a hurdle. He didn't tell many people that story, because even now the trip down memory lane hurt. But Nya was different.

Chapter 15

"That's the house?" Nya asked. "It's gorgeous!"

The house was a ranch-style home that had been kept up immaculately. The grounds were beautiful, with thick green grass, well-trimmed shrubs and colorful flowers bordering the driveway. There was a wooden swing on the front porch, giving the place a homey feel. It was exactly the kind of dream home Nya had always wanted.

She turned to Tyler as he parked the car. "This place is beautiful."

"It is. And John's parents are great people. They love hosting parties because they've got the space."

"I can imagine."

"I suspect they're very happy that John is back with Suzie and that they're finally gonna tie the knot."

"Hopefully, he still loves her."

"I think he never stopped," Tyler said. "He made a bad decision, but he couldn't run from his feelings for Suzie."

"I guess they were meant to be," Nya said. Then she looked at the house and drew in a deep breath.

"You nervous?" Tyler asked her.

"A little," she admitted. "I hope your friends like me."

"There's no need to worry. This is a good group of people, and everyone's friendly."

"And Carol?" Nya held his gaze. "Do you know if she'll be there?"

"I haven't talked to her, but I imagine she will be. Get ready to smooch with me in the pool." He grinned.

Smooch in the pool... Nya was already thinking about doing a lot more than smooching. It was amazing that just being in the car with Tyler made her feel so sexually alive. And she didn't think it was just because they'd had a seriously hot night, nor the fact that she'd been celibate for months.

No, she was certain that it had everything to do with the fact that she liked Tyler...more than she wanted to.

The sound of happy chatter and laughter made it clear that all of the activity was happening at the back of the house. Tyler, obviously knowing his way around, opened a side gate, and they entered the backyard.

A group of people lined the curvy pool area, and across from them a young girl went down a water slide and landed in the pool with a splash.

The wooden deck was large and spanned almost the length of the pool. A couple dozen people were on the deck, some standing, some sitting. Most of them had either a glass of wine or a bottle of beer in hand, and smiles all around.

"Tyler!" A man who'd been leaning against the deck's wrought-iron railing quickly bounded down the steps. As he reached Tyler, he threw his arms around him and gave him a hearty hug. "So glad you could make it."

"Of course," Tyler said. "I wouldn't be anywhere else." Then, facing her, Tyler said, "This is Nya. Nya, this is John, one of my best friends growing up."

John gave her a bright smile. "Hello." As he shook her hand, a mischievous look came over his face. "I see you've been doing well for yourself," he told Tyler.

Tyler slipped his hand around Nya's waist. "What can I say?"

"Well, you look happy, and you definitely deserve to be happy."

Tyler gazed into Nya's eyes. "Thanks."

Nya swallowed. She didn't know how much of what Tyler was saying was an act for John. Or for Carol. She glanced around the backyard, wondering if Carol was there.

"Come on," John said. "Let's get you a drink. Nya, you want a beer or some wine? Or something else?"

"What's the something else?" Nya asked.

"My dad's making margaritas."

"Oh, sure. I'll have a margarita," Nya told him.

They made their way up onto the deck, where a few lounge chairs were available. Tyler gestured for her to sit, and she did.

"I'll get that drink for you," he told her.

Nya nodded, though she wanted to tell him that she would go with him. She looked around and saw smiling faces. A woman who was sitting in a lounge chair across from her offered her a big smile and waved.

"Hi," she said. "I'm Christine. You are?"

Nya returned the smile. "I'm Nya."

"Are you Tyler's girlfriend?"

Nya hesitated. Then she said, "Um. Yeah."

"How long have you been together?" Christine asked.

"Not very long," Nya answered, feeling slightly uncomfortable. She knew that she was playing a charade, and answering questions made the charade more difficult. She and Tyler hadn't discussed what they should and shouldn't say about their relationship.

She was glad when he made his way back over to her.

"Hey, babe." He handed her a margarita that looked delectable. "Here you go."

"Thank you, sweetie."

Tyler stroked the back of her neck, the kind of intimate gesture that couples shared. She drew in a steadying breath as a tremor of desire shot through her body. How was it that he was so darn irresistible?

Tyler sat on the lounge chair beside her. "Christine. Good to see you again."

"Likewise," Christine said. "It's been a while." Her eyes volleyed to Nya. "I met your new girlfriend."

"Nya, Christine is John's sister."

"Ahh," Nya said. "Your parents have a beautiful place."

"Thank you," Christine said.

Nya looked toward the man at the grill. "Something smells good."

"You're in for a treat," Christine said. "My dad is grilling up some steaks with his special sauce. They're to die for."

"He must be really happy that John's getting married," Tyler said.

"He's already talking about grandchildren," Christine said.

Tyler chuckled. "I'll bet." Then he stood and offered Nya his hand. "Let's make the rounds. I want to introduce you to everybody."

Nya took his hand, and they went down to the main level of the backyard. She met Suzie and some of Suzie's family, but so far, Tyler hadn't mentioned Carol.

"Carol's not here?" Nya asked softly.

"I don't see her."

"You think she's coming?"

"I'm not sure." He encircled her in his arms. "But

even if she doesn't show, word will get back to her that I was here with someone and that I'm happy. So it's still a win-win."

Nya stared up at Tyler, suddenly wondering just how in love with Carol he had been. And it was weird, but she actually felt a little jealous. After all, he had obviously loved Carol deeply. They'd been engaged.

"You haven't really told me about Carol," Nya said.

He gave her an odd look. "You want to know about my ex?"

Nya shrugged. "I mean, if you want to tell me..."

"The first batch of burgers is ready!" John's father announced, interrupting the moment between Nya and Tyler.

"You want a burger?" Tyler asked her.

"Definitely."

"Looks like we just lost our seats on the deck," Tyler said. "Why don't you snag those two chairs over there, by the pool? I'll get your burger."

He offered her a small smile, passed her his beer then turned and started off. Nya watched him go. And saw him falter about four steps into his walk. He paused.

Nya quickly looked in the direction of his line of sight and saw a beautiful woman. She was wearing a black shirt and crocheted white skirt and had rows of white-and-black beads around her neck. She was slim, with fair skin and a mass of thick, curly hair.

Carol.

It had to be. Tyler's physical reaction gave it away.

She was gorgeous. And perhaps irrationally, Nya was jealous. Again, she wondered just how into Carol he had been. And even more, she wondered why they had broken up.

Tyler started to walk again, but he didn't head to the

grill. Carol, who'd been on the far side of the backyard, was walking toward him, and Tyler made his way over to her.

Nya watched, almost not breathing, as the two met. They greeted with an awkward hug, and Nya's stomach tightened.

Of course he has to talk to her, Nya reminded herself. Just as she had spoken to her ex at the premiere.

Tyler and Carol spoke for about a minute, then Tyler continued on to the deck where he got a couple of burgers. Not a moment too soon, he was heading back over to her. "One burger for you," he said, passing her the plate.

"Thank you."

Tyler sat in the chair beside her. Her gaze fell to his muscular outline. Tyler was a gorgeous guy, and he seemed genuinely sweet. Had Carol actually walked away from a man like Tyler? And if so, why?

"That was Carol," he told her.

"That's what I figured," Nya said.

As Tyler looked at her, something in his gaze suddenly changed. Out of the blue, he was stroking her face. It took her a moment to realize that he was in performance mode for Carol's benefit. And when he leaned across the chair and kissed her, Nya knew that was for Carol, too.

And she hated it.

Was this how Tyler had felt when she'd had him play the doting boyfriend? Suddenly, the idea of pretending to be his girlfriend left her feeling unsettled.

Tyler stroked her cheek then kissed her again. A soft and lingering kiss that caused an electrical charge to course through her entire body.

But the warmth was instantly followed by a sensation of cold as she reminded herself that the kiss was just part of the act.

Tyler broke the kiss and eased back, offering her that charming smile. God, he was an amazing kisser.

Tyler took a bite of the burger. "Mmm. It's good. Take a bite."

As Nya sampled the burger, her stomach tensed. Her birthday with Tyler had been incredible, but she could feel the wall creeping back up. Suddenly, she was remembering all of the advice from her support group, and she knew they would tell her that falling into bed with Tyler had been a huge mistake. That having sex had clouded the issue, and put her at risk of heartache.

She saw Tyler's gaze wander in the direction of his ex, and she felt another spate of jealousy.

"You like the burger?" Tyler asked.

"It's great," Nya said. Though the truth was, all she could taste on her tongue was bitterness.

Was Tyler over his ex? Or was there still something lingering between them?

"She's definitely noticing us," Tyler said.

Nya forced a smile. "Good."

Nya finished her burger then reached for her margarita. She was tempted to gulp it down, but she took a couple of moderate sips.

"Hey, Nya. Are you going in the pool?" Christine asked as she walked over, now wearing a white bikini.

"Um, I'm not sure."

"I'll get your bag from the car," Tyler said. "We can both go in the pool."

"Awesome." Christine beamed. "We're gonna play water volleyball."

Tyler got to his feet. "I'll be right back."

Tyler headed to the car, and Christine sauntered over to the pool. Nya was glancing around when she saw Carol, in a stunning gold bikini, exit the house.

Good Lord. A part of Nya wanted to head to the car and tell Tyler that they should leave. The idea of Tyler setting his eyes on Carol in that skimpy bathing suit bothered her.

But he didn't seem to notice Carol as he made his way over to her with her tote bag. He also had her camera bag in tow.

Nya stood to meet him. "Where shall we change?"

"In the house. I'll take you."

He put his arm around her waist and led her to the downstairs bathroom. When Nya exited Tyler was already in his suit, waiting for her.

She sucked in a breath. That body…his muscular arms, that washboard stomach. She felt a sexual charge as she checked him out.

But when she saw the way he was looking at her, the sexual charge intensified. His lips were parted, and he looked at her with an expression of wonder. "You are so beautiful."

Nya blushed. "Thanks."

"You always look away when I tell you that," Tyler said. "Sometimes I wonder if you know how beautiful you are."

"I…" Nya started to speak but then stopped. Tyler was right. People hadn't told her that often. Not even boyfriends. And especially not Russell. "I guess I'm not used to hearing it."

"Well, you look gorgeous. That bathing suit is hot."

It was a red bathing suit with white bows at the side. And the way Tyler was looking at her made Nya wish she could slip into the bathroom and have Tyler take it off her…

"There you are!"

Nya jerked her gaze to the left and saw Christine. "Yep. Here I am."

"Wow! That's a gorgeous bathing suit."

"I was just telling her the very same thing," Tyler said.

"What were you two about to do? Hook up in the bathroom?" Christine flashed them a playful yet suspicious grin. "You've got all night to spend with her. But right now, she's needed in the pool."

Christine was clearly one of those women who liked to make instant and fast friends. Nya didn't mind. She was happy that Christine liked her.

Christine linked arms with her and led her out of the house. When they made it to the pool's edge, Nya looked over her shoulder. She saw Tyler checking her out, and heat flooded her body.

"You're gonna be on my side," Christine announced. "Tyler, you go on the other team."

Nya watched Tyler get into the pool on the other side. That's when she noticed Carol was on that side.

Tyler winked at her, which set her mind at ease. But as the game began, Nya couldn't help noticing that Carol took every opportunity to get close to Tyler.

When the ball went in Tyler's direction, Carol threw herself in his direction. Yes, she was trying to get to the ball…but was she also trying to get to him?

And when Carol high-fived Tyler after their side scored, then linked fingers with him for a prolonged moment, Nya wanted to scream.

"Come on," Christine said to her. "Get your head in the game. Yes, Tyler is gorgeous. But we're gonna lose if you keep checking him out."

Nya tried to concentrate on the game, and when the ball came toward her, she smacked it back over the net. It was heading straight for Tyler, but Carol vaulted herself in front of him. Her body collided with his, and the two of them plunged backward into the water.

As Carol righted herself, she giggled like a little schoolgirl. And Nya knew then, without a doubt, that Carol wanted Tyler back.

Chapter 16

The game of volleyball over, Nya swam beneath the net and went over to Tyler. She looped her arms around his neck and kissed him.

"Mmm," Tyler moaned.

Pulling back, Nya threw a glance in Carol's direction. Carol was looking over her shoulder, watching Nya and Tyler intently.

"I'm getting changed," Nya told Tyler. "Are you staying in the pool?"

"No, I'm getting out. Why don't you take some pictures?" Nya opened her mouth to say no, but Tyler said, "You'll be awesome."

Drawing in a shuddery breath, Nya nodded. Tyler's faith in her evaporated her nerves. "Okay."

"What?" Tyler asked, giving her a questioning look.

"I was just thinking… Probably I shouldn't tell you what I was thinking."

One of Tyler's eyebrows rose. "Hmm. You have me intrigued."

"I was just…imagining taking some…interesting pictures of you."

Tyler's tongue flicked over his bottom lip, a purely suggestive gesture. "I like what you're thinking," he said, his voice husky. "And later, I'll be all yours. But first, get some pictures of everybody."

She pulled her bottom lip between her teeth, loving the flirtatious vibe between them. "Okay."

Nya started out of the pool, throwing a glance at Tyler over her shoulder. She gave him a sly look.

She wanted to make love to him again.

He followed her out of the pool, but as she got her bag with her towel and clothes, John and Suzie came over, and Tyler began to talk to them.

Inside the house, Nya dried off and got changed. She'd take some pictures, then she and Tyler would leave and go back to her place. Why not?

The more time she spent with Tyler, the more she believed that he wasn't going to hurt her. And that was a good feeling, because it was so hard to resist him.

Nya looked at herself in the mirror. Her hair was wet, so she pulled it into a ponytail because there was nothing else she could do with it. The pool had washed the makeup off her face, and she actually liked herself this way better. She looked fresh-faced and younger.

Feeling sexy and vibrant, Nya went back to the party. She halted when she saw Tyler standing below the deck talking to Carol. Carol threw her head back and placed a hand on Tyler's chest.

The wave of jealousy Nya felt was intense. And it was quickly followed by anger. Why was Tyler standing there with Carol? Wasn't he supposed to be changing?

What was the point of bringing someone to a party to play your girlfriend if you were going to get all chummy with your ex?

Trying to keep her emotions under control, Nya went over to Tyler and Carol. "I thought you were getting changed, sweetie." Nya gave Tyler a look of mock reproof. Then she turned to Carol. "Hi." She extended her hand. "I'm Nya."

"I'm Carol." Though she smiled at Nya, there was an undertone in her eyes. A look that drove home the point that yes, she obviously still wanted Tyler.

"You and Tyler are dating?" Carol asked.

"Yes." Nya slid her arm around Tyler's waist. "And I understand you used to date him."

"We used to be *engaged*," Carol said, as if it were very important for her to relay that fact to Nya. Carol looked at Tyler, a soft smile spreading on her lips. "Not all that long ago, actually. Just about five months."

Nya wasn't going to play this game. So she said, "Babe, why don't I get a picture with you and John?"

"Oh, you're taking photos?" Carol's eyes lit up. "Take a picture with me and Tyler."

Nya swallowed but stepped backward. Carol quickly took her place at Tyler's side, slipping her arms around his waist. She beamed, and Nya took the picture.

Tyler stepped away from Carol, saying, "I'm glad that new business venture is working out. I'll talk to you later."

He put his arm around Nya's shoulder, and they walked over to John. But Nya was still irritated, and there was no question as to why.

Glancing over her shoulder, she once again saw Carol looking at them.

Sizing up the competition...

If the relationship was truly over in Carol's mind, she would've done what she could to assuage any insecurities Nya might have. She would've assured her that their relationship was in the past, and that there was no rekindling it. But she hadn't.

"John, my man," Tyler said when they reached him. "Let's get a picture. Nya's a photographer."

John's eyes lit up. "Oh, really? Maybe Suzie and I can talk to you about our wedding?"

"I..." Nya's first inclination was to say no, that she was just a hobbyist. But instead, she said, "If you like the pictures I take tonight, we can talk about it."

John threw an arm around Tyler, and Nya snapped a few photos of them. Then she made the rounds, taking pictures of John's father at the grill, happy people in the pool and the other party guests. People were happy to pose, and she even took some photos of John and Suzie with the hillside and ocean as their backdrop.

"I love these!" Suzie said. "Honey, maybe one of these can be our engagement photo?"

Nya beamed. They really liked the pictures that much?

Nya glanced around, looking for Tyler so she could tell him the good news.

He was nowhere to be seen. It took her no more than a few seconds to realize that Carol wasn't around, either.

Moving quickly, Nya headed into the house. She went down the hallway that led to the bathroom. That's when she heard the voices.

"...his new girlfriend?"

"It doesn't sound that serious to me. It's only been a few months."

That was Christine's voice.

"I don't know." Nya recognized Carol's voice. "I'm trying to gauge how he feels, but I'm not sure."

"I didn't get the sense that Tyler and Nya are deeply in love," Christine said. "Besides, how can their relationship compete with what you and Tyler had? You two were together for three years. I'm sure he still loves you. Look at my brother. He and Suzie broke up. Now they're getting married. Your history with Tyler is something that neither of you can ignore."

A lump lodged in Nya's throat, and she tried to swallow it away. But it remained. Turning on her heel, she headed toward the patio doors, not wanting to be spotted by Christine or Carol.

As she stepped outside, she felt a wave of emotion. Christine had been so nice to her during the evening. And now Nya knew why. She had gotten close to her to try to see how big of a threat she was for Tyler's affections.

Nya spotted Tyler on the deck, talking to John's parents. She went over to him. "Sorry to interrupt."

Tyler looked at her, smiling warmly. "You're not interrupting. Everything okay?"

"Actually, I'm not feeling well," Nya said. "Can we leave? Tyler, do you mind?"

"Of course not. Let me just say goodbye to everybody."

"Can I have the car keys?"

Tyler looked at her with concern. "It's that bad?"

"Yes."

"Here." He dug them out of his pocket and passed them to her. "I'll just say bye to John and Suzie, then."

Nya said her goodbyes to the people in her path as she hustled to the far side of the backyard and escaped through the gate. She felt angry and betrayed and so emotionally out of sorts that she could cry.

When she got into the Lincoln, she sat down and drew in a deep breath. A couple of minutes later, Tyler joined her in the car.

"You really don't look good," he said. "You want me to stop somewhere, pick something up for you?"

"I just want to go home," she said, an edge to her voice.

"What's wrong?"

"I'd just like to get home."

Tyler started to drive, and after a couple of minutes of silence, he asked, "Are you upset with me?"

Nya exhaled sharply then faced him. "Seems to me that you and your ex aren't through with each other."

Tyler's eyes bulged. "Excuse me?"

"Are you really going to pretend that you couldn't see it in her eyes? And you didn't do anything to help her think that you're over her."

"What are you talking about?"

"I thought you brought me there because you wanted to prove a point to her? Instead, it looked like you were busy rekindling your feelings for each other."

Tyler looked perplexed. "Obviously, we were going to speak. We're not bitter enemies. But it was clear that you and I were together."

Nya scoffed.

Tyler frowned as he looked at her again. "If you don't tell me what's wrong, how can you expect me to guess?"

"Because we were both at the same barbecue. And if it was obvious to me, it should be obvious to you."

"Carol was talking to me for a bit about her new business venture," Tyler explained. "She's opened up a smoothie bar with a friend."

"You practically spent more time with her than you did with me. And good grief, could she have been more all over you in the pool? The whole point of a fake girlfriend, by the way, is to spend time with the fake girlfriend. Like what we did at Russell's event. We couldn't keep our hands off each other then. Tonight, it was like you were forcing it, which made it all too clear to me that your feelings for Carol are still firmly in place."

A beat passed, and Tyler's eyes said he didn't agree. "Actually," he began, "I think the exact opposite happened. I think everyone who saw us had no doubt that we were into each other."

Nya wanted to tell him what she'd heard Christine say but decided not to. This wasn't about Christine.

"Wait a second," Tyler said after a long moment. "Are you jealous?"

"Jealous?" Nya scoffed. "I'm embarrassed. You made a fool of me in front of your friends."

"Friends you will never see again," he pointed out. "Is that really why you're upset?"

"Of course you wouldn't understand."

Suddenly, Tyler was jerking the car to the side of the road and parking in front of a random house. "What don't I understand?"

Nya looked at him. "I just want to go home, Tyler."

"So you don't even want to talk about this?"

She said nothing.

"Clamming up and not saying anything doesn't solve the issue. Yes, I was involved with Carol, but it's over. I don't know if you're feeling jealousy—"

"I feel disrespected," Nya said.

"Disrespected?"

"Yes, disrespected," Nya reiterated. "Carol was flirting with you, right in front of my face—and you did nothing to stop it."

Tyler stared at Nya, wondering why they were even having this crazy argument. And yet, it gave him hope. Because if Nya were actually jealous, then that meant that she cared.

"Carol and I haven't seen each other since we broke up. We broke the ice, and it was good to be friendly. But that's all we were…friendly."

Nya pouted, and Tyler couldn't help it. He smirked. Even angry, she was still so darn cute.

She glared at him. "You find this funny?"

"Admit it," he said. "You're jealous."

"Are you still in love with your ex?"

"Would it matter to you if I were?"

Nya's eyes flashed, and even her nose seemed to flare.

"I'm not saying that I am," Tyler quickly said. "But damn it, Nya, if you're going to be upset with me, at least admit that it's because you care."

A few beats passed, then Nya groaned. "I can't believe we're having this conversation."

"I agree," Tyler said. "Let's move past this."

Nya faced Tyler. "Look, what happened between us on my birthday…it was—"

"Amazing," Tyler supplied.

"A mistake."

Tyler frowned. "What?"

"Our being together was…a reaction."

"Hell, yeah, it was a reaction. It was a reaction to being attracted to each other."

"It was a reaction to it being my birthday, and how well the evening was going, and…and we just kind of went with the moment."

Tyler stared at her, not understanding. "You didn't have any regrets until tonight."

"That's because tonight…" Nya exhaled sharply. "Tonight, it became clear to me that we both moved too fast. Carol's not through with you yet—"

"Carol dumped me. I was going to marry her, and she dumped me."

Nya was silent. She watched him, but Tyler couldn't read what was in her eyes.

"That doesn't make me feel better. If she's the one who dumped you—"

"She sped up the inevitable," Tyler said. "Yes, I was planning to marry her. But long before we broke up, we were no longer truly connected. We hadn't made love in months." Tyler stared at Nya, not sure if he was getting through to her. "Our relationship was going to end one way or the other. Especially once I learned from a mutual friend that she'd hired someone to spy on me to see if I was cheating. She'd drop hints here and there about other women. I always assured her that I loved her. I didn't make the connection between her lack of trust causing us to drift apart until after we broke up and I learned she'd actually paid money to have me followed. Despite me being a devoted fiancé, she didn't trust me. That hurt me deeply."

"Did she have reason not to trust you?" Nya asked. She shrugged, adding, "Sometimes people are very flirtatious and cause others to feel insecure."

"Fair enough," Tyler said. "But that's not who I am. When I'm with someone, I'm with them. Spying on me, checking up on me—it really gets under my skin. I extend my trust, and I expect the same in return. If there is no trust, then there is no relationship. The worst part is, she never got any proof that I was anything other than faithful…and she *still* dumped me. There's no going back to Carol."

Nya nodded slowly, and Tyler wasn't sure what she was thinking. He understood having emotional ties to someone else that were hard to cut, but that wasn't the case with Carol.

"Honestly," he went on, "Carol is not even an issue here. I like you, Nya."

She was shaking her head. "We've got chemistry.

That's obvious. But what happened between us…it's not what I wanted."

"Ouch." She could have fooled him.

"I mean, I'm taking a break from dating. I mentioned that. And what I'm feeling now…well, it's clear I made a mistake by jumping into bed with you too soon. I created this artificial situation that put us together, and we took it too far."

"I have no regrets, Nya."

Nya faced him, her expression conflicted. "But I do."

Tyler felt as though someone had just hit him in the gut with a baseball bat. She regretted what had happened between them? A sense of disappointment more profound than Tyler was prepared for washed over him.

"Let me start over," Nya began. "I…I don't regret what happened. Honestly, it was amazing. I loved every moment of it. And that's exactly the problem. Just *how* much I loved it."

Tyler frowned. "I don't see the problem."

"The problem is that I always fall hard and fast," she said, not meeting his eyes. "And it's done nothing but leave me brokenhearted. I need to do things differently."

"So you want to take things slowly?" Tyler asked, for clarification.

"Actually, before meeting you, I had sworn off men."

"Forever?" Tyler asked, aghast.

"No, not forever. Just…for several months. Maybe a year."

"And how long has it been?"

"About six months," she said. "I'm trying to focus on me…please try to understand."

Tyler didn't understand. But by the way she wouldn't meet his eyes, he knew that he couldn't pressure her into changing her mind. Maybe she was just upset about

Carol, though God only knew why. She'd had him pretend to be her boyfriend for Russell, so they'd been through this situation already.

"I promised myself that I would take a significant amount of time to get in touch with myself and to concentrate on me and what I want. To love myself and know that I'm okay without a man."

"You need time? That's what you're telling me?"

"Yes."

"Okay." Tyler tried to hide his frustration and started to drive once again. He'd hoped that they would end the night in his bed, but apparently, that wasn't going to happen.

Twenty minutes later, when he was pulling up in front of her house, Nya turned to him. "I don't want you to be mad at me. I just…I just don't want sex to cloud my judgment."

"Do me a favor? Don't mention sex again."

"I…" He saw her swallow. But thankfully, she didn't say anything else about wanting him but *not* wanting him. She wanted space, and he would give it to her.

Because it wasn't just sex he wanted from her, and he wanted her to know that.

Nya opened the door, and Tyler also got out to walk her to the door. She looked over her shoulder at him, and in her eyes he saw a mix of emotions.

"It's all right," he said softly. "I know there's something between us, Nya. So I'll give you time. Because you're worth the wait."

Her lips parted, and Tyler thought she was going to say something. But before she could, he pressed his lips to her forehead.

"Good night, Nya."

Then he turned, got back in the car, and disappeared down the road.

Chapter 17

Five days, and no word from Tyler.

Nya was more upset about it than she wanted to admit.

I know there's something between us, Nya. So I'll give you time. Because you're worth the wait.

As he'd left her standing on her front step, Nya had so badly wanted to tell him that she'd changed her mind. That she wanted him to go upstairs with her. But she'd said nothing, and he'd walked away.

Now, every day since then, she'd found herself wanting to call him. All she wanted was to hear his voice. But she knew she'd already been a confusing mess, and she didn't want to call and add to his confusion.

If she called him, she wasn't sure she could resist begging him to come over.

Nya was surprised when she got a text from John Friday after work. He'd explained that he'd gotten her number from Tyler and was interested in seeing the pictures from the engagement party.

The fact that Tyler hadn't called her directly about this hurt her on some level…and yet Nya knew she didn't have a right to be hurt. She was the one who'd pushed him away.

She'd sent him the best pictures she'd taken of him and Suzie. It took no more than thirty minutes for him to send her a message saying that he loved the pictures and wanted to talk to her about ordering some wedding announcement cards with one of the photos.

Shocked, Nya called him. "Hello, John. This is Nya."

"Hey, Nya. Suzie and I loved the photos. Are you able to make some Save The Date cards for us using one of the images? Maybe we can meet, and you can break down the cost for us?"

"Um…sure. How about Monday? I work with a photographer, Sabrina Crawford. She's the one who did the firefighters' calendar."

"Ah, yes. I've heard of her."

"Do you have any time on Monday? I can call you in the morning and schedule a time for you to come in to the studio to go over package options."

"Awesome," John said. "Tyler highly recommended you as a photographer, so I'm looking forward to this."

Nya was momentarily stunned. "I'll talk to you Monday, then," she said, injecting confidence into her voice.

As Nya ended the call, a warm sensation filled her. Tyler had highly recommended her skills as a photographer? He didn't even know what she was capable of.

And yet, for him to say that meant that he was expressing high faith in her abilities.

She wanted to call him…

Instead, she got her laptop and her camera bag and left the house. She knew that Sabrina was spending the evening with Mason, and Nya didn't want to be home alone. At least at her favorite coffee house, she would feel as though she were out and being social. Afterward, she might take some photos of the bay at night.

Ten minutes later, she was at the café, which was alive with activity. Most of the comfy armchairs were taken, but the small, two-person table in the corner of the coffee shop was available, and Nya was glad. She'd come to see it as her spot.

She ordered a decaf coffee so that she wouldn't stay up all night then signed online to her support group. She found a few of her friends were online and chatting.

TRYINGMYBEST: I totally fell off the wagon. I met this guy, and I can't believe I slept with him. Nine months into my born-again virginity, and he seriously tempted me. The worst part is, I don't even know if things will work out between us.

ANDBRAINSTOO: Don't beat yourself up. It happens. You're human. The point is, you've decided not to continue to live a life of constant casual sex. We can't always be perfect.

GUYSWANTLOVETOO: It's really hard when everything you see on TV and in ads is all sexualized. I'm trying to be good, trying not to have any relationships. But I know what it's like to miss the sex.

THEONLYWAY: Don't excuse what she did. It's wrong. She broke her own sacred vow.

GUYSWANTLOVETOO: Just saying I understand the temptation. The funny thing is, when you suddenly take yourself off the market, that's when girls seem to want you more.

ANDBRAINSTOO: Always the way.

THEONLYWAY: Trying, you need to make sure that you

stop all contact with this guy! Tell him it's over, and that you never want to see him again!

Nya poised her fingers over the keyboard, ready to write something in defense of TRYINGMYBEST. This wasn't the same as being an alcoholic. There was no reason that you had to completely abstain forever. But THEONLYWAY, who was the administrator of the group, seemed to believe that the only way to succeed in life was to forget your sexual side altogether.

THEONLYWAY: You've come so far. I can't believe you blew it.

MAKING_ACHANGE: Don't beat yourself up. You're not the only one who messed up. I did, too.

THEONLYWAY: What? You, too?

MAKING_ACHANGE: I didn't plan it. It just happened.

THEONLYWAY: The guy you were lusting over in the picture? Why didn't you stay away from him?

MAKING_ACHANGE: It happened, and I take responsibility for it. I also learned from it.

THEONLYWAY: I'm disappointed in both of you.

Nya rolled her eyes.

RESPECTME1: Well, I have good news. Bill proposed! I'm engaged!

There were a number of congratulations and well-wishes. Except from THEONLYWAY.

THEONLYWAY: Are you still waiting until your wedding night?

RESPECTME1: Yes. He's been very understanding. In fact, he thinks that waiting until our wedding night is exciting. He's totally shown me that he's the right guy!

There were more congratulatory messages from the group.

Nya sipped her coffee, wondering what Sabrina would think of the group.

As she lowered her mug, her eyes connected with a guy across the coffee shop. She'd seen him before. Several times, in fact. Like her, he came in alone and spent time on his laptop.

The guy smiled at her. Nya quickly looked away. She didn't want to give the guy the impression that she was interested in him.

But to her horror, he walked over to her. "Can I join you?"

"Um…" Nya didn't want to be impolite, but she also didn't want to encourage him. "I was just about to leave, actually."

"Oh."

Nya quickly downed her coffee and stood then closed her laptop. "Yep."

"Can I get your number?" he asked.

"I'm involved with someone," Nya told him. She stuffed her laptop into its carrying case then started for the door.

As she stepped outside, she glanced over her shoulder. Saw through the window that the guy was back at his table.

Thank God.

But when she settled behind the wheel of her car, she noticed that he was now exiting the café. He started right for her car. "I'd just like to take you to dinner."

Nya backed out of her parking spot, perhaps a little too quickly. She'd already told the guy she wasn't interested. Why was he following her out?

"Come on," he yelled, kicking the back of her car.

Nya flinched when she heard the thud. Was the guy insane? He had just kicked her car!

Nya sped out of the parking lot and onto the street. Her car went over part of the sidewalk in her haste to get away. She heard a scraping sound, then her small Fiat 500 bounced as it hit the street.

At the light where she would normally turn left, she quickly turned right. Then she turned right at the next corner, not knowing where she should go. She only knew that she didn't want the guy from the café to follow her. Which meant she couldn't head home, on the off chance that he was able to track her down by her vehicle.

Nya made another turn and ended up on Mountainview Road. That was the street that led up into the hills of Ocean City. She followed the same path Tyler had taken when they'd gone to John and Suzie's engagement party.

And soon, Nya's anxiety was ebbing away. Looking down at the view of Ocean City was incredible. She loved the way the city was lit up at night, and the way the moon glittered on the dark ocean. She found a spot to park and took a moment to catch her breath and relax.

Just like Tyler had said, the drive up the hillside was calming.

Tyler… Why was she fighting so hard to keep him out of her life?

The answer came to her in a nanosecond. Because she was afraid of getting hurt. And she just *knew* that Tyler was the kind of guy who could decimate her heart.

She wanted to call him.

Instead, she sighed and started her car. But as she began to drive, she noticed something odd. There was a weird whooping sort of sound, and the car felt like it was sloping to the right.

A flat tire? Nya wondered.

She stopped the car and got out to have a look. Sure enough, the front right tire was flat.

"Damn it," she muttered. What was she going to do now?

Tyler… His name sounded in her mind.

Going back into her car, she retrieved her phone from her purse and called him. God only knew what he was up to. It was a Friday night, and he could easily be out for a night on the town.

Maybe even with another woman…

An image of Carol purposely colliding with Tyler in the pool caused her stomach to tense. What if he was out with Carol?

"Stop being so afraid and call him," she told herself. She needed him.

Tyler picked up after two rings. "Hello?"

"Tyler, hi." Pause. "It's Nya."

"Nya." She could hear his exhalation of breath. "How are you?"

"Actually, I'm not doing so good."

"What happened?"

So she told him. Told him about the creep at the coffee shop, and how she must have hit something in the road because she now had a flat tire. "And now I'm on Mountainview Road, and I have a flat tire. I know it's Friday night, and you're probably out, but I didn't know who else to call."

"Where exactly are you?" Tyler asked.

"Just past the corner of Driscoll."

"Wait inside your car. I'm on my way."

As the call ended, a soft smile touched Nya's lips. She didn't know if Tyler had been out on the town, or at home alone. But whatever he'd been doing, he was dropping everything to go to her.

The next fifteen minutes seemed like hours as she waited for him to arrive. And when his Lincoln came up the hill, relief overcame Nya. She'd needed someone, and he'd come to help her, no questions asked.

As he pulled up in front of her, Nya exited the car. Tyler opened the driver's-side door and got out.

He was dressed in jeans, a pale pink dress shirt and black loafers. And with the backdrop of the city behind him, he looked larger than life…and sexier than ever.

Her real-life sexy hero.

"Hey," he said, walking toward her. "Are you all right?"

Nya nodded. "Just a bit shaken up."

He hugged her, but it was too brief for Nya's liking. And then it struck her. Tyler had come to help her, but he was being guarded. Guarded because she had told him she wanted time.

He walked around to the front of her Fiat to examine the damage. He bent onto his haunches, and the headlights from his car highlighted the way his thigh muscles flexed. *Good Lord…*

"Your right tire is definitely flat," he said, "but it also

looks like you have some front-end damage." He glanced up at her. "Did you collide with something?"

"I went over the curb pretty hard. I was trying to get away from that lunatic."

Tyler stood to his full six-foot-two-inch height. "The guy actually kicked your car?"

"Yeah. At the back." Nya wandered to the back of her car. The scuff on the rear panel showed where the guy had kicked it.

"Son of a…" Tyler's voice trailed off.

"All I did was tell him that I wasn't interested in dinner," Nya said then wrapped her arms around her torso. "I wasn't mean, I wasn't rude…"

Tyler cradled her in his arms. "It's not your fault. Lord knows there are some seriously crazy people out there."

"I'd seen him plenty of times at the coffee shop. He's never approached me before, much less gotten aggressive."

Tyler smoothed a hand over Nya's hair then released her. The moment their bodies were separated, she missed his warmth.

"You have a spare tire on this car?" Tyler asked. "Man, it's tiny."

"Actually, there's a compartment under the car that houses the spare," Nya explained.

Tyler pursed his lips. "This is going to have to go to the shop. I know a guy with a body shop. I can call him and have him tow it there."

"Oh, that would be great."

"Then I'll get you home."

Nya's stomach twisted. She didn't want to go home. At least not alone.

Tyler headed toward his car, and Nya got her camera out of the backseat of her car before joining him in the

Escalade. He had already called the tow truck when she got into the passenger seat beside him.

"My friend said a truck will be here in about twenty minutes."

"Thanks."

Silence filled the car, and Nya felt nervous. Here she was with a guy she was crazy about, and it was like they had a glass partition between them.

"Maybe you ought to call the police," Tyler said. "Give them a description of that guy."

Nya shook her head. "I don't know… I guess I probably just won't go back there anymore."

"Which gives him control over your life."

"Maybe tomorrow," Nya said. "Right now…I just want to decompress."

"I'll get you home as soon as that tow truck shows up."

Nya swallowed. "Sorry to drag you away from whatever you were doing. Looks like you were out."

"I was out with some of the guys from the station. Having a couple of beers. No big deal."

"Well, thanks, anyway. I appreciate that you came to help me right away."

"Of course."

Lord, Tyler smelled good. And it was hard to *not* check him out. His hard body, his handsome face…everything about him was so darn appealing.

Facing him, Nya said, "About getting me home… I… I don't want to be alone tonight." And then she cringed, fearing Tyler would think she was crazy.

When she opened her eyes, she saw him looking at her curiously. "Are you saying you want me to go home with you?"

"I…" She drew in a deep breath. "Yes. Or we could go to your place."

Nya saw him swallow. "Nya…you made it very clear that you weren't interested in pursuing a relationship."

"I know. But… God, Tyler. Being in this car with you… All I can think about is spending the night together."

"There's no doubt there's chemistry between us, Nya."

"It's not just the physical chemistry. Every time I think I can push you away and forget about you, I can't. And then I see you again, and…I feel like I'll die if you don't touch me."

A rumbling sound emanated from Tyler's chest. Damn it, why was she doing this to him? He was trying to give her space, give her another five months if that's what she needed. But when she talked about needing him to touch her, how could he resist her?

"You've had a rough night," he said.

"That's not the reason I want to spend the night with you," she said. "Heck, Tyler. From the moment I sent you away last week, I regretted it. And I know…I know you think I'm a hot mess."

He stared at her, at her beautiful face. At those expressive eyes that were filled with need. He knew what she was feeling, because he was feeling it, too. Whenever they were in the same space, it was as if a magnetic force was drawing them together.

"I don't think you're a hot mess," he whispered, leaning close to her. She edged her face closer to his, and then he claimed her lips in a hot and heavy kiss. A desperate moan escaped from her mouth, and she dug her fingers into his shoulders, making it clear just how much she needed him.

"Nya. You're making me crazy, you know that?"

"I'm sorry," she whispered then moved her lips to the

underside of his jaw. And God help him, he wanted to take her right there in the car.

"When we're together, there's this inexplicable kind of passion that makes me lose all sense of reason. And I'm through fighting it."

Somehow, Tyler found the strength to pull away from her. "But that's not what I want. For us to have another amazing night, and you run again, telling me it was wrong. Damn it, Nya. What I'm feeling for you isn't only physical. I've told you before…I like you."

Nya eased her head back and gazed up at him, a smile touching her lips. "Tyler, if you knew what I was feeling…"

"Tell me," he rasped.

She drew in a breath, her full bosom rising and falling in a way that made it hard for Tyler to concentrate on anything other than the lust flowing through his veins. Why was his attraction to her so incredibly fierce? He hadn't even felt this way about Carol.

He slipped a hand around her waist and pulled her as close as he could. "Tell me," he whispered into her ear.

She mewled. "What I'm feeling for you… The feelings have been hard and fast. And that's why I'm so scared." She paused, looking into his eyes. "Because I'm falling for you, Tyler. And I can't stop myself."

Tightening his hand on her waist, he grinned. "I'm feeling the same way. And yes, it's scary. But I don't want to run from it."

Just as Tyler was about to kiss her again, the tow truck pulled up behind Nya's car.

"Damn," he said. He tried to adjust his aroused member.

Cute baby bunnies, he told himself.

Chapter 18

With Nya's Fiat towed away, Tyler turned to her on the street and said, "My place is closer. You want to go there?"

Nya grinned at him. Then she offered him her hand. Taking it, he led her to the car.

Always a gentleman, Tyler opened the passenger door for her. Once she was seated, he leaned in for a kiss. Though it was short and sweet, it took her breath away.

She wanted more.

Tyler held her gaze through the window as he rounded the vehicle then got in beside her and started to drive. There were no words. And none were necessary. All Nya could think about was what was to come.

Another amazing night with Tyler.

No more excuses. No more turning back.

Why did she want him so desperately? What was it about him?

Reaching across the seat, Tyler took her hand in his and gave her a small smile.

Suddenly, it was clear to her why she was drawn to him like a moth to a flame. He had a sincere quality she had never found in another man she'd been interested in. She didn't see just lust in his eyes; she saw affection.

And she knew he would always be there for her. Even

though she'd pushed him away, he had still come to help her.

As Tyler continued to drive, the passion between them was like a third passenger in the car. Nya was desperate for his fingers on her body. Moving their joined hands to her lap, she placed his hand on her inner thigh.

His eyes shot to hers, and they widened with delight. She edged his fingers higher.

"Nya," Tyler said hotly.

"Touch me." She put his hand higher, getting ever nearer to her sweet spot.

"Are you trying to make me crash the car?"

"I'll die if you don't touch me."

So he did, gently stroking her outside of her jeans. It wasn't nearly the way that Nya wanted him to be touching her, but it was the best he could do with her jeans on.

His fingers went up and down, and Nya threw her head back and moaned.

This wasn't like her. To be acting so desperately needy, as if her life depended on his touch.

And yet, something about Tyler made her want to lose all inhibitions and give herself completely to pleasure.

He stroked her again, and she whimpered. Then his hand went lower, skimming her inner thighs gently, before taking her hand in his again.

"I need to concentrate on driving, or we'll never make it to my place."

Nya's chest was heaving with ragged breaths.

"Don't worry," he said. "We're almost there."

Nya had time to notice that Tyler lived in a ranch-style home with a two-car garage. She had time to see that he had a large lawn in pristine condition. But once he led her through the front door, she barely registered the modern furnishings before he pulled her into his arms and began to kiss her.

Nya moaned into his mouth and slipped her arms around his neck. She had her camera bag hanging over her shoulder, and Tyler maneuvered it off her arm. Then, encircling her waist with both arms, he walked with her into the living room.

Gently, he bit her bottom lip, and Nya gasped. He moved his lips to the underside of her jaw, where he trailed the tip of his tongue along her skin and up to her earlobe. When he drew her earlobe between his lips and then nibbled on it, Nya's knees buckled, and she clung to him as sensations swept over her.

His hands smoothed down her back and then crept underneath her shirt, all while his tongue flicked over her earlobe. Prickles of pleasure spread from her ear, down her neck and over every inch of her body, awakening all of her erogenous zones.

As Tyler's mouth found hers again, his hands moved to the front of her body. He squeezed the mounds of her breasts as his tongue twisted with hers.

"Oh, Tyler…" Nya moaned. The fact that she had ever resisted him, resisted this, seemed insane.

"I know, baby."

He pulled her T-shirt over her head, dropped it onto the floor then made quick work of undoing her bra. As her breasts spilled free, he covered them with his hands and then began to tweak her nipples into hard tips.

"You are so beautiful." He dipped his head and flicked his tongue over one nipple then twirled it around her areola. The pleasure was so intense, Nya could die from it.

Tyler's lips went to her other breast, and he gently bathed that nipple with the heat of his tongue before drawing it into his mouth and sucking on it slowly. Nya dug her fingers into his shoulder blades and held on, because her body was so weak with need that she couldn't sustain her own weight.

When his mouth left her breast, Nya sighed with disappointment. But he was soon moving his lips down her torso, planting slow, hot kisses along her flushed skin. When he got to her belly button, he gripped her hips tightly and dipped his tongue into the groove.

Then he quickly unbuckled her jeans and dragged them down her thighs, his mouth still on her abdomen. "Sit down," he said softly, his breath warm against her skin.

Nya backed up to the sofa, where she sat. Tyler then knelt before her and pulled her jeans down and tossed them aside. She saw his eyes lock on her panties, and she felt a sexual charge knowing that the sight of her body was turning him on. He slipped his hands along the sides of her panties and began to pull them down. Nya eased her hips up so that he could have easier access.

His eyes met hers, and they were darkened with desire. Then he touched her nipple, and Nya pulled her bottom lip between her teeth. She was on the sofa, naked before him. Completely vulnerable.

She'd never wanted anything more than she wanted this.

She shuddered when Tyler's lips went to her inner thigh. His fingers trilled her skin as his lips moved higher and higher. And soon, all she could do was arch her back as his lips and tongue began to tantalize her most sensitive spot.

Nya was lost in a sea of pleasure. Tyler's touches were filled with care. She knew that what he was doing with her wasn't strictly about lust. It was about something more.

She stroked his head and said, "Please, baby. Make love to me."

Tyler kissed his way back up her abdomen, between her breastbone, ultimately reaching her lips. She felt cherished when he linked his fingers with hers and kissed her slowly, hotly and deeply.

And then he stood before her and stripped off his shirt, his eyes on hers as she watched him get naked. He took his time, as though to torture her with the sweet pleasure of anticipation. And when he slipped off his boxers and his arousal sprang free, Nya gasped. Oh, how she wanted him...

She thought he would take her right there and then, but he reached for her hand and pulled her naked body against his as she stood. Gently framing her face, he kissed her again, reminding her of the words he had said to her.

I like you, Nya.

She liked him, too. She more than liked him...

Pulling apart, he took her hand and led her across the cool floor to a bedroom on the right side of the house. He guided her to the bed, and she lay on it as he went to a drawer and retrieved a condom. Nya checked out his naked form, that firm and delectable behind. Physically, he was all a woman could hope for.

And emotionally, he was proving to be the same.

He joined her on the bed and wasted no time settling between her thighs. He kissed her, slipping his tongue into her mouth at the same time as he guided his erection inside her.

Nya moaned long and loud as he filled her. With each stroke, she felt closer to him, as if their souls were truly connecting. Her entire body came alive with the most delicious sensations.

But that didn't compare to what she was feeling in her heart.

She knew that despite her vow, and despite the short time she had known him, that she had fallen for him.

And this time—unlike other times—something in her gut told her that he was her Mr. Right.

A soft clicking sound caused Nya to stir. She opened her eyes and realized that she was between the sheets of an unfamiliar bed.

Tyler's bed.

She heard the clicking sound again, and recognizing what it was, she quickly rolled over. She saw Tyler sitting on the side of the bed, holding her camera.

He'd been taking pictures of her.

"What are you doing?" she asked.

"This is a nice camera." Tyler put the camera to his eye and snapped another photo of her.

Nya threw her hand outward, as though that could block the path of the camera's lens. When he snapped yet another picture, she covered her face with both hands and whimpered. "Please don't. I must look hideous."

"Hideous? You look stunning. With your hair rumpled, and your sleepy eyes…you still look amazing."

Nya separated her fingers and peered at Tyler. "You always say the sweetest things."

"I mean it. And it's not just me who knows it. The camera loves you, too."

"I don't think I'm that photogenic."

"I disagree." He turned the camera around so she could see the screen. "Look."

Nya did. She laughed when she saw the picture he'd taken of her with her hands in front of her face. There was something spontaneous and cute about it. He went to the previous picture, one of her form under the sheets as she slept. It captured a warm essence of the morning after a great night in bed. The next picture was of her when she'd been sleeping. There had been the hint of a smile on her face. Her happiness and contentment had radiated through the camera's lens.

"You're right. They are beautiful." She smiled at him. "Hmm… If firefighting doesn't work out for you, looks like you can have a career in photography."

Tyler put the camera on the night table and slipped into bed beside her. "I took the liberty of checking out some of the pictures on your memory card."

Nya felt a spasm of alarm. The night they'd made love at her house, she had snapped a photo of him while he'd been sleeping. He'd been lying on his stomach, his butt exposed.

"Please tell me you didn't."

"Yeah," Tyler said, his expression saying he didn't understand what the big deal was. "Are you upset?"

"I just…I kind of hate anyone else looking at my pictures until I'm ready to show them."

"Why? Because you don't think you're good enough? Well, I think you've got what it takes. I was very impressed."

Just how far had he gone into her gallery, and how much had he seen? Had he seen—

"I saw that picture you took of me," he whispered.

Nya cringed. "I'm sorry. I hope you're not mad."

She hadn't set out to take a nude shot of him. But the sheets had only been partially covering his body that night, and he'd looked so darn gorgeous. She knew she should have asked him if it was okay to keep it once he'd woken up, but she hadn't.

"I… You just looked so good, and I took the picture.

But it's not like I plan to put it on my wall or anything. I just…I just kind of wanted something to keep of you that was uniquely mine."

"Don't apologize," Tyler said, his voice husky. "I was surprised but also flattered. A little more risqué than what I took for the calendar, but I still liked it." He stroked her cheek. "And I like that you wanted something to keep of me."

Nya's wariness ebbed away. "You make a perfect subject, by the way."

"I'll pose for you anytime you want."

She drew in a deep breath, feeling arousal begin to stir.

"Speaking of pictures," she began, "I heard from John. He and Suzie loved the photos." Nya ran her hand along his arm, a sense of pride filling her chest. "They loved them so much they want to use one for a wedding announcement. And they're actually going to come into the studio on Monday to discuss ordering an entire wedding package."

"That's fantastic!" He kissed her.

"I'm shocked but elated," Nya said. "But I don't know if I should be the one to do the pictures. Sabrina is the expert, and we're talking a wedding here."

"Which isn't happening for several months. It will give you time to hone your craft. I know you can do it, babe."

Nya smiled up at him. "Why do you have so much faith in me?"

"I just do."

She was warmed by his words. Snaking an arm around his neck, she gave him a lingering kiss. When she pulled back, she asked, "Why did Carol dump you?" When Tyler met her eyes, she continued. "I mean, you just seem so incredible. You're sensitive, gorgeous. An all round great guy. Who walks away from that?"

"She had her reasons, I guess. Ultimately, we weren't meant to be together." Tyler smoothed a hand up the side of her torso then covered her breast. "Are you complaining?"

Nya beamed at him. "Not a chance."

"Good."

Planting his lips on hers, he eased her body backward on the bed. And as he kissed her and touched her body, Nya hated that they couldn't stay in his bed forever.

Because all she wanted was Tyler in her life.

Chapter 19

The next couple of weeks were heaven for Nya. She got together with Tyler as often as their schedules allowed, and they made love as if they were training for some kind of new sporting event. It felt good to be giving herself to a guy she was crazy about, and who was also crazy about her.

And her career aspirations were finally taking off. With John and Suzie interested in photos, Nya had shown Sabrina the pictures she'd taken of them, and Sabrina had been impressed.

"When did this happen?" she had asked.

Nya had shrugged. "I've kind of been interested in photography for a while."

"Why didn't you tell me?"

"I…I thought you'd think the idea was crazy."

Sabrina frowned at her. "Why? You know I'm going to need help to keep up with demand. Having you as a partner would be ideal."

"Really?"

"Of course. You know I'll show you the ropes, help train you as you need it." Then Sabrina had hugged her. "Nya, this is awesome."

"Tyler's the one who insisted I bring my camera to that party," Nya had said. "He believed I could do it."

"Seems Tyler has been great for you in a lot of ways."

"I'm so happy. But on one hand, I'm scared. What if all of this is too good to be true?"

"Don't let fear hold you back, sweetie. Seriously, I've never seen you happier. I've seen you excited and hopeful about a lot of guys before, but this is the first time I've seen this true light in your eyes. I never saw that when you were with Russell."

"Really?"

"Hundred percent."

Nya had felt encouraged by Sabrina's words, and by her faith in Nya's potential. Sabrina had insisted that Nya be the one to do the photos for John and Suzie's wedding.

So as the weeks passed, she didn't let negative thoughts hinder her happiness. She finally decided to live in the moment.

When Nya received Tyler's text about coming over to discuss Thanksgiving plans, she beamed. Thanksgiving was around the corner and spending the holiday together meant that they were ready to take the next step in their relationship.

She drove straight to his house after work. Every time she saw his large home, she thought of the fact that he lived in a house meant for a family. A wife and a few kids.

She noticed something different as she parked in the driveway. The dying shrubs that had been lining his driveway had been replaced with flowers. Two days ago, the shrubs had still been there, and he'd worked yesterday. When had he gotten the time to do some gardening?

She made her way to his door, and before she could even knock, he opened it. He beamed at her, which warmed her from the top of her head to the tips of her toes. He always looked at her as though his life was now complete because she was in his presence.

"Babe," he said, and pulled her into an embrace. He kissed her lips softly. "I missed you."

"You got enough rest?" she asked him.

"Don't you worry." He winked at her. "I'm rested."

"Looks like it," Nya said, stepping out of his embrace. "You got up and did some gardening today?"

Tyler didn't answer right away, and in those silent moments, Nya picked up on something. Something that caused her body to tense.

"Actually, Carol planted those."

"Carol?"

"She came by of her own volition yesterday. I had no clue. She left me a note, telling me that she planted the flowers."

The floor seemed to sway beneath Nya's feet. "You've been talking to Carol?"

"She's contacted me a couple of times." Tyler shrugged. "It's no big deal."

"She planted flowers in your garden," Nya said. "It seems like a big deal."

"She said she wanted to do something nice for me."

And Tyler believed that? Or was he playing the incident down for her?

Nya knew what was happening, and she hated it. Carol was trying to make inroads again. Trying to be sweet and generous so that Tyler would fall for her again.

But Nya let the matter drop. *Tyler's with you now,* she assured herself.

And she felt confident about that.

That night, after they'd made love and fallen asleep, she heard Tyler's phone beep.

It was three in the morning. Who sent someone a text at three in the morning?

Nya glanced in Tyler's direction, but he hadn't heard his phone. He was breathing heavily and still in deep sleep.

Nya could no longer sleep. She had a guess about who it was, and she had to find out if she was right.

Carefully, she got out of the bed. Tyler still didn't move. She crept around to his side of the bed and picked up his phone from the night table. Then she tiptoed into the en-suite bathroom and closed the door. Sitting on the edge of the bathtub, she looked down at Tyler's phone as if she were holding a bomb in her hands.

Nya pressed the button to wake his phone from sleep mode, and sure enough, the message on the screen was from Carol.

I can't stop thinking about you.

Nya's stomach twisted.

Tyler didn't have a password on his phone, so Nya had no trouble getting in. She quickly accessed his text messages. And she felt sick as she read his dialogue with Carol. There were five other messages, each one progressively worse.

CAROL: It was great talking to you yesterday. Thanks for your new number. It's much easier to communicate this way.

Tyler had given her his number?

TYLER: I was definitely interested in some of those ideas you presented.

A couple of days had passed before there was another message from Carol, and this one made Nya's stomach twist painfully.

CAROL: I still love you, Tyler. Please, can we talk?

And Tyler's response, which made tears fill Nya's eyes, read:

Let's meet at the Health Nut Smoothie Bar at 1 PM tomorrow.

CAROL: I'll be there! :) xoxo

Nya's tears dropped onto the screen of Tyler's phone, and she wiped them off with her pajama top. Tyler was meeting Carol.

The truth she'd read had shattered her world. Worse than it had ever been shattered before.

Because she'd come to love Tyler more deeply than she had ever loved anyone.

He'd won her over with his sweetness, his compassion, and his belief in her. And when she'd finally surrendered her heart to Tyler, Nya had wholeheartedly believed that he was not like other men. The past six weeks with him had been an incredible ride, and she'd believed with every fiber of her being that she had found her forever love.

How had she been so wrong?

You have no clue what he's going to say to her, a voice in her mind said.

But the woman had come by and planted flowers at his house, for God's sake. She was fixing to move in. That much was clear.

To think that she'd been sleeping with him for weeks…

and now he was about to talk to Carol about reuniting with her.

Sadness gripped her heart as she remembered what Christine had said to Carol. She had all but assured Carol that the love she and Tyler had shared wasn't dead, that he would move on past Nya and reunite with her. Just like John and Suzie had.

More tears filled Nya's eyes. Damn it, Christine had been right.

Nya forced herself out of the bathroom. She returned Tyler's phone to his night table and slipped back into bed beside him. But what she wanted to do was flee. Leave him to wake up and wonder where she was and why she'd left.

But she had a better plan. She would have the last laugh.

Turning onto her side, she tried not to cry…but the pain of Tyler's betrayal hurt more than any other pain she'd ever known. Even when Russell had ended things with her, she'd known in her heart that it would have happened sooner or later. She'd just lied to herself. She had seen how Russell had flirted with Topaz and other women, so the fact that he'd cheated on her hadn't been any big, shocking surprise.

But Tyler…he had portrayed himself as loyal.

"Everything okay, babe?"

Nya was surprised by his question and flinched when he slipped his arm around her waist. "I just went to the bathroom," she said, managing to keep any emotion out of her voice. "Go back to sleep."

He pulled her close, and she settled against his body.

She had specifically asked him about Carol, and he'd told her that there was nothing between them anymore. He hadn't even mentioned meeting with her when she'd brought up the flower planting, which Nya saw as a huge red flag.

And now he was going to meet her to talk about getting back together...

The only reason Nya wasn't leaving his bed was to see how he dealt with this situation in the morning. What would he tell her?

A plan was formulating in her mind. A plan to confront him and Carol. She wanted him to know—and Carol, as well—that she wasn't a fool.

But fool or not, her heart was hurting. Because she had dared to love again.

And it was crushing her to know that Tyler didn't love her back.

Chapter 20

The next day, Tyler was as sweet as usual to Nya, preparing her boiled eggs and a plate of fresh fruit for breakfast. He'd gotten her into jogging with him in the mornings, and she'd built up her stamina over the past few weeks to where she could now jog two miles. As a result, her body had become more toned. So many positive changes had happened to her since she'd been involved with Tyler.

And now, it was about to be over.

"Babe," he said, placing a hand on her hip as she dipped her head back and drank from her water bottle. "I have a couple of errands to run this afternoon. Feel free to stay here if you like—"

"Actually, I have some stuff to do, too," she said, managing somehow to keep her voice light. "It's laundry day. Plus, I want to do some test shots at Bay Gardens."

"Great," Tyler said. "That's a great plan."

"If I'm going to be serious about taking pictures, I need as much practice as I can get."

"Absolutely. You're a real photographer in the making."

Nya swallowed as she looked at Tyler. Even now, he was still so supportive, still always saying the right thing. She felt a niggling of doubt about not trusting him. So she asked, "What will you be doing this afternoon?"

"I've got to head to the hardware shop, get some supplies for the deck." He shrugged. "Take care of a few things."

Grief smacked Nya in the face, but she tried to bite back her emotion. How could she have been so foolish as to believe that things would be different with Tyler? Hadn't all of her relationships proved to her that when it came down to it, men couldn't be trusted?

She snatched up her purse from the hall table. "I'm gonna get going."

She turned to head out of the house, but Tyler quickly took hold of her arm and forced her to face him. "Aren't you forgetting something?" he asked.

She shook her head, confused.

"A kiss."

"Oh." She forced a smile. "Of course."

He kissed her, and Nya had to fight not to cry. She was able to keep the tears at bay until she was behind the wheel of her car.

Tyler had had the opportunity to tell her about his meeting with Carol. But he hadn't.

Which told her everything she needed to know.

In the two hours that passed before the big showdown, Nya tried to summon her anger, not her tears. She had been screwed over by far too many men. And if Tyler was just like the rest of them, he didn't deserve her tears.

She was nervous, sickened, scared to death at the idea of confronting Tyler. And yet, for her own peace of mind, it had to be done. Because she knew that if she simply brought the issue up with Tyler, he would possibly lie, or tell her she was mistaken…and she would *want* to believe him. She would want to ignore her brain and trust her heart.

And she was tired of doing that. She'd done it with Russell, only to be heartbroken in the end. No, the only way to deal with the issue was to catch him with Carol— where he wouldn't be able to deny the truth.

"Why, Tyler?" Nya asked as she watched the clock tick down in her apartment. She had told him about her fear of falling too hard, too fast. Her fear of being heartbroken. Yet he'd romanced her, anyway.

Maybe he'd simply come to realize that he still had feelings for his ex. But why not just tell her the truth face-to-face? That would hurt less in the long run.

Nya didn't understand. Tyler was thoughtful and romantic and cared about her career. He certainly presented himself as a man who would respect her enough to be honest with her.

But she'd given him a chance to tell her about Carol, and he hadn't.

Their connection had been real, hadn't it? Yet after all of that, he was going to go back to his ex?

Nya drove to the Health Nut Smoothie Bar and parked far down the street so Tyler wouldn't spot her car. Tyler and Carol were due to meet at one, and it was now twelve minutes after the hour. They should both be inside by now.

Nya drew in a deep, anxious breath. *Do it,* she told herself.

As she walked, she felt as though she could retch. On one hand, she knew she had betrayed Tyler's confidence by going into his phone. She expected that he would be mad about that. But she wouldn't have looked through his messages if Carol hadn't texted him at three in the morning. If she hadn't seen Carol's words on the screen.

If she hadn't planted those stupid flowers.

And to think that Nya had given up on her vow of celibacy because she'd believed Tyler was her Mr. Right. She could only imagine what THEONLYWAY would have to say about what she had done. She had stopped visiting the online support group once she and Tyler had become so heavily involved.

Nya cursed under her breath when she saw that the entire front facade of the smoothie bar was windows. She wouldn't be able to sneak up and not be seen.

Thankfully, there was a bit of a foyer before going into the restaurant at large. Nya peered around the corner, her eyes sweeping the place frantically for any sign of Tyler and Carol.

Pain ripped through her heart when she spotted them at a table near the back.

She jerked her head back to stay out of view and sucked in a breath. Nya had come here for this. And yet she wasn't prepared to see them together.

Get it over with, she told herself. Then, with purpose, she started toward the back of the restaurant. She was glad that Tyler's back was to her so he didn't see her coming. And Carol's eyes were on Tyler, so she didn't notice Nya until she was at the table. When Carol saw Nya, her eyes widened with surprise. Realizing that something had gotten Carol's attention, Tyler glanced over his shoulder, and a look of shock came over his face.

"How dare you have lied to me?" Nya demanded.

Tyler was regarding her as though he couldn't believe she was there. "Nya?"

"You told me that I was special. That you cared about me."

Tyler got to his feet. "Nya, what are you doing here?"

"What am I doing here? What are *you* doing here?"

Nya's gaze went to Carol, whom she now noticed had red-rimmed eyes. Had she been crying?

"It's not what you think," Carol said.

"Don't say a word to me," Nya snapped. "I overheard you at the engagement party, plotting to get Tyler back."

Nya could see that Tyler was looking beyond her, at the other patrons in the restaurant. She glanced over her shoulder, saw curious eyes staring in their direction.

She wasn't yelling and screaming, but clearly people could see that there was a confrontation going on and were suddenly interested in the drama unfolding before their eyes.

"Can I talk to you outside for a moment?" Tyler asked. He spoke through gritted teeth, and Nya knew that he was not happy.

"There's really nothing you can say. I just came here to let you know that I'm not a fool. And I will not be played for a fool. If you wanted to get back together with your ex, you should have just told me, instead of sneaking around behind my back."

"Outside." Tyler took her by the arm, clearly embarrassed.

He led her out of the restaurant. Nya glanced at some of the gawking patrons as she passed them. Tyler might be mad at her for embarrassing him in this way, but she was even more mad at him for lying to her.

As soon as he whisked her outside, Nya pulled her arm free of his grip and met his eyes with an angry gaze. "I know you're upset that I showed up like this, but you told me that you and Carol were through. Yet you're meeting her behind my back?"

"How did you know I was going to be here?" Tyler asked.

The question caught Nya off guard. There was only one way for her to have known that he would be here.

"You went through my phone?" His disappointment was palpable.

Nya said nothing, but stuck her chin out defiantly. He wasn't going to turn this around on her. "I didn't plan it. But when your phone went off at three in the morning with a text from your *supposed* ex… Yes, I needed to see what she had to say. Then I find out you two are reconciling, and you can't even be honest with me?"

"I can't believe you," Tyler said with disgust.

"You can't believe *me*? You're the one on a date with your ex!" Nya's voice faltered. "You two are reuniting, and you keep sleeping with me? I thought you were different."

"Carol and I are not reuniting."

"I saw her texts, Tyler. And I saw yours."

He folded his arms over his chest. "Really? And what did I say?"

"You agreed to meet! If you weren't interested in reuniting, you would have told her no, that you weren't going to meet with her. From the time I saw the flowers, I knew there was something going on. You blew it off like it was no big deal, but my gut told me I couldn't quite believe you. Every guy has always lied to me. *Always.*" Nya tried to catch her breath. Emotion was overcoming her. It was because she cared so much. She cared about Tyler more than she thought possible. And she'd believed him when he told her that he cared about her, too.

For him to turn out to be just like other men who had lied to her, deceived her…

"Yes," Tyler began, and it was clear that he was trying to keep his anger under control. "Carol called me. Said she wanted me to invest in a new smoothie shop she wanted to open. I was willing to consider the idea. After that she texted to say that she was still in love with me and that she wanted to meet. So I agreed to meet her. Because I needed to make it clear to her face-to-face that there was no longer an *us*. That I'd met someone else I was crazy about, and I had moved on."

Nya's stomach bottomed out. She couldn't even speak; she just stared at Tyler as the breath oozed out of her.

Had he just said what she thought he'd said?

As if to emphasize exactly what Tyler had told her, Carol came out the door and said without preamble, "I'm sorry, Nya. You're upset, and you're obviously thinking the worst." She blew out a weary breath. "I met with Tyler behind your back. And yes, I wanted him back. But it's clear I was misguided. Because he loves you." Carol wiped at her tear-filled eyes. "Sorry for going behind your back. I didn't mean to hurt you. I just wanted him back because I realized I was a fool to let him go."

Nya stared at Carol, a sense of guilt and horror overwhelming her. She'd jumped to conclusions.

The wrong ones.

"Oh, God," Nya whispered.

"I just wanted you to know," Carol said. "Because I know how it looks. But you have nothing to worry about. I'm sorry I caused you any pain, but one thing I can tell you about Tyler—he's not the type to have an affair." Carol looked at him, tears falling onto her cheeks. "If he's with you, he's with you. You can trust that. I threw away a great guy."

Nya didn't know what to say. But she noticed that Carol was wearing an apron that said HEALTH NUT on the front.

Carol brushed away her tears then said to Tyler,

"You're right about not wanting to invest in the second shop. It's a bad idea. I'm going to get back to work."

Then she turned and went back inside.

When Nya looked at Tyler again, she saw that he was staring at her with disappointment.

"I'm sorry," Nya said. "I just—"

"Save it."

"Tyler, I'm sorry. But I overheard Christine and Carol at that party, plotting to get you back in Carol's life. And then she was at your house, planting flowers. I just... I felt insecure. I didn't mean to spy on you. I'm sorry."

"You should have trusted me. Without trust, a relationship can't survive."

"I wanted to. But so many guys have lied to me before."

"I'm not other guys."

"I asked you what you were doing this afternoon. You weren't honest with me."

"Because I wanted to take care of this, make sure Carol understood we were over before I spoke to you about it. I didn't want you to worry needlessly."

Nya whimpered.

"I've done nothing to earn your distrust, Nya. I've tried to encourage you. I've offered you my love. But clearly, you don't want it."

Nya took a step toward him. "That's not true, Tyler."

He put up a hand. "Stay away from me."

His words were like a stab to her heart. "Tyler. I know I was wrong. I was scared. So darn scared because I care so much about you."

"You should've come to me. Instead of coming to this restaurant to humiliate me in front of all these people."

"I know. Please just try to understand my frame of—"

"I'm done," Tyler said, shaking his head. "I've been

there for you the best way I know how. And I didn't do anything to deserve what happened today. You don't trust me, and I can't deal with that. So I'm done."

"Tyler."

Turning on his heel, he started to walk away.

"Tyler."

He didn't stop.

"Tyler!"

Nya started toward him. "Tyler," she said as he went to his driver's-side door. "Tyler, please."

He turned and faced her. "Don't bother."

His words stopped Nya in her tracks, and the tears came then. Tyler wasn't going to hear her out. He wasn't going to forgive her. For him, it was simply over.

She watched him start his car and drive away. And as he did, her heart shattered.

She loved him. Loved him dearly. That was why she'd had her insane reaction—she couldn't stand the thought of losing him. But now he was leaving her life.

Forever.

Chapter 21

Nya was devastated. She'd lost Tyler. And the worst part was, she'd brought it on herself.

You should've talked to me. That was what Tyler had told her. And it was something she had considered, but she'd dismissed the idea because she had feared he would lie to her.

Men had lied to her before—too many times—and she hadn't been able to trust her own judgment.

All she had wanted was Tyler's love…and to know for certain that she had it. Ironically, Carol's words had made that clear.

But now Tyler no longer wanted her.

Oh, God. How could she fix this?

I'm done.

The look of disillusionment in his eyes had said it all. There was no going back for him. Nya had blown it.

On Monday morning, Nya woke up for work, but she couldn't muster the strength to get out of bed. So she texted Sabrina and told her that she had a doctor's appointment in the morning and wouldn't be in until the afternoon.

Sabrina's response had been typical. *If you don't feel well, don't worry about coming in today.*

Nya crawled back under the covers and stayed there

for a very long time. But after a couple of hours, all she'd accomplished was to deepen her depression. She needed a friend. And not those faceless people online who would give her ridiculous advice about her life when they didn't really know her.

She needed Sabrina.

So Nya dragged herself out of bed and went to work at noon, when she knew Sabrina would be taking her lunch break. And sure enough, she found her in the kitchen taking out a salad from the fridge.

"Sabrina."

Sabrina began to turn. "I told you not to come—" Her words died in her throat when she took one look at Nya. "Nya, sweetie. What's wrong?"

"I..." Nya sniffled.

Sabrina put her salad down on the counter and opened her arms to Nya. Nya walked into her embrace. "Nya, what is it? Did you get bad news at the doctor?"

"I didn't go to the doctor."

Sabrina eased her head back to look at her. "My God, are you worried something serious is going on? Look, you have to go to the doctor. You need to know for sure."

Nya shook her head. "I'm not sick. I—I did something yesterday. And I ruined everything!"

Sabrina's eyes narrowed in confusion. "What did you do?"

Nya explained what had happened. About the flowers, and Carol's text in the middle of the night, and how she'd decided to confront Tyler and Carol.

"Except he was meeting Carol to tell her that he loved *me* and that they would never be getting back together. Now he thinks I don't trust him, and he said he's done with me."

"Oh, Nya."

"I tried to make him understand, but he's never going to forgive me. He said he didn't deserve my distrust, and that our relationship won't work. I know what I did was wrong, but don't you think he should understand my point of view?"

Sabrina rubbed Nya's back. "Nya, why didn't you talk to me first? At the very least, I could have talked to Mason. Gotten a read on whether Tyler still had feelings for his ex. They're friends, remember? Mason would have told me the truth."

"I didn't even think about that. I just… I told you what I heard Christine saying to Carol. And when I saw those flowers, and saw her texts…what was I to think?"

Sabrina said nothing, but Nya imagined that her friend was thinking that she had taken drastic actions. And that those drastic actions had led her to this very situation. But Sabrina would never tell her that. Because Sabrina was a good friend. The kind who would support her regardless of the mistakes she'd made.

"Do you want me to talk to Mason?" Sabrina asked. "Maybe I can get him to convey to Tyler the state of mind you were in. Just how hurt you've been and the fact that you were just scared. Scared to trust. Maybe he'll understand."

Nya's heart lifted at the idea, but she also knew it would be a cop-out. "No," she said. "I have to be the one to make him understand. To make things right. I have to make him understand that I'll never ever betray his trust like that again."

Sabrina nodded. "You're right. And I think that will mean a lot, coming from you. He loves you, Nya. I'm sure he'll find it in his heart to forgive you. After all, no one's perfect. He shouldn't hold this against you forever."

Nya wanted to believe that. But she also knew that Tyler had seemed fed up. Done.

What she hadn't told Sabrina was the fact that Tyler had once confided in her that Carol had never fully trusted him, and how that hurt him deeply. And now she had exhibited the same trait.

Nya had been worried about her own insecurities, not realizing that Tyler had his, as well. Maybe because of what she'd done, he no longer believed that he could completely trust women.

Oh, God.

The more she thought about it, the more she feared that Tyler would *never* forgive her.

But she had to try.

The next day, Nya wrote Tyler a heartfelt letter. She explained to him her insecurities, took responsibility for her actions and promised him that if he gave her the chance, she would never betray his trust again. Never again would she jump to conclusions and not ask questions. She ended the letter by telling him that she loved him. And all she wanted was a chance to prove to him that she could be a girlfriend he could trust.

She personally delivered the letter to the firehouse. And then she waited, almost losing her mind as the hours ticked by with no response from Tyler. The next morning, she saw she had a text from him. She quickly opened the message, unable to breathe until she'd seen what he had to say.

Got your letter. Thank you. The truth is, I didn't handle the situation the best way. I didn't tell you about Carol, which led to your suspicion. So I share the blame for what happened.

Nya's heart filled with hope—until she read Tyler's next words.

However, the fact remains that you wouldn't have known about the meeting if you hadn't gone into my phone. Nya, without trust we can't have a relationship. Initially, you said you needed time. Maybe things between us moved too fast. Now I think you need some time, and me, too, to get some clarity on whether we should give things a second shot.

Nya's stomach bottomed out as she read Tyler's text. She reread it, analyzing each word. It was clear to her that Tyler was ending things, but letting her down gently.

Still, as the rest of the week went by, Nya kept hoping that he would reach out to her. Tell her that he wanted to see her. But after a week, there'd been nothing.

Nya was trying to keep it together, but her heart was broken, and she felt a sense of loss so profound that she didn't know how she would get over it. She thought that she'd loved Russell, but Russell had never really inspired the same kind of deep emotion that she'd felt for Tyler. With Russell, she'd always felt she wasn't quite good enough, and he had done everything to encourage those feelings.

But Tyler had tried to make her realize that she had all the potential in the world. That no dream she could ever have was too big.

Every night before she went to sleep, Nya lay in bed, barely able to keep herself together.

Had she been her own hindrance to happiness? Had her fear that she wouldn't find love led her to destroying the very love she'd found?

About a week after the text from Tyler, she came to

a stunning realization. All those years she'd spent desperately trying to find Mr. Right had been fueled by the belief that she was never good enough.

Tyler had summed up her fear of pursuing what she loved—she didn't exactly believe in herself. She had let her naysaying parents and others convince her that her dreams were foolish and unattainable. She'd accepted their doubt without ever truly fighting to prove that she could succeed.

Until this moment, she had believed that attitude had only extended to her career aspirations. Now it was clear that it had also extended to her relationships.

And it suddenly occurred to her that she was handling the Tyler situation with the same expectation of failure. She'd written a letter to apologize to him, owning up to what she'd done wrong. And she'd hoped that he would call her to talk.

He hadn't, and very likely it was because a letter wasn't enough. She needed to do something more.

She had to show him that she'd learned and changed and grown.

She had to show him that she loved him and deserved a second chance.

The next day, the Monday before Thanksgiving, Nya woke up knowing what she would do. She couldn't simply accept that Tyler wouldn't forgive her. It was time that she go to see him. Make him understand face-to-face that she was remorseful and that she had learned a lot from the incident.

Nya knew that he was at work today, so she would go see him around lunch, maybe bring him some food. There was a deli close by that he loved.

Yes, she would bring him one of his favorite sandwiches. And then she would lay her soul bare. Make herself completely vulnerable to him.

When Nya got to work, Sabrina greeted her as she had every day since her breakup with Tyler. With concern brimming in her eyes, Sabrina asked, "Did you hear from Tyler?"

Nya shook her head. "No."

"I'm sorry, hon. I was hoping that at least over the weekend, he'd reach out to you."

Nya was done feeling sorry for herself. She was through playing the victim. She had created her current circumstances, and it was up to her to resolve the situation.

"I made a decision." When Sabrina looked at her with curiosity, Nya continued. "I've been waiting for Tyler to come to me. For him to decide when we've had enough time to figure things out. But the truth is, *I* screwed up. Yes, I wrote him that letter, and I would've loved nothing more than for him to come running in here and tell me that he forgives me. But I'm not gonna sit around waiting for him to do that. I love him. I write one letter, and I call it quits? That's hardly any effort at all, is it?"

Sabrina smiled.

"I'm going to see him. Prove to him that I'll always trust him. Prove to him that I love him. I don't need any more time to figure things out. Every moment without him, my world is falling apart. I want him back." Nya nodded, knowing that her decision was the right one. "And I'll go see him every day if I have to, until he believes me. And only when I know—absolutely know—that he no longer loves me, then I'll give up."

Sabrina's smile grew into a radiant beam. "Good for you. And girl, it's about time."

Hugging her torso, Nya drew in a breath. "I'm terrified. But I have to do this."

"I'm proud of you."

Nya was feeling positive for the first time in eight days. Her decision felt right. She would only give up on Tyler when she was convinced that he no longer had any feelings for her.

She could hardly wait for lunch to arrive. But at 11:00 a.m., the news came that a fire was raging in downtown Ocean City. And at 11:20 a.m., Sabrina came rushing up to the reception desk.

"What is it?" Nya asked her.

"A firefighter from Station Two was killed in the fire!"

Nya jumped to her feet. "What?"

"I can't reach Mason, and I don't know if he's okay..."

"Tyler," Nya whispered.

Dread flowed through her veins. God, no...

What if Tyler had been killed before she'd had the chance to prove that she loved him?

Chapter 22

Terrified, both Nya and Sabrina left the studio to head to the scene of the fire. A meat packaging plant was burning, and the news reported that it was a five-alarm blaze. A firefighter had been killed, several had been injured, but no names had been released.

Sabrina was beside herself. So was Nya.

As Nya drove, she also prayed. Prayed that just when she had seen the path to getting her man back, he wouldn't be taken away from her.

God, please don't let Tyler be gone. Don't let him be gone before I've been able to tell him just how much he means to me. And please let Mason be safe. Lord, don't let him be hurt.

As they neared the scene of the fire, police had barriers up, blocking access to the street.

The flames were massive, and thick black smoke was billowing into the sky.

"Oh, God," Sabrina whimpered.

In the distance, Nya could see the row of fire trucks with ladders extended and a number of firefighters hurrying around. At least four ambulances were parked on the street, and Nya wondered if more than one person had been killed. The fire looked that devastating.

Sabrina got out of the car and ran to the barrier. The

police officer held up a hand to keep her at bay. Nya got out of the car just as the officer said, "You can't go past here, miss."

"A firefighter was killed. Do you know his name?" Sabrina asked.

"I have no information, sorry."

"My boyfriend is a firefighter. He's from Station Two, and his shift is on right now."

"I'm sorry," the officer repeated. "I've got no information about who's been injured or killed."

Sabrina's face collapsed, and Nya went over to her and took her into her arms. Together, they both cried. Nya prayed even harder for Tyler and Mason.

"Come on," she said to Sabrina, turning her toward the car. "We can't go down the street. All we can do is head back to the studio and wait for news."

Back at the studio, Nya and Sabrina were glued to the television in the reception area. Sabrina had sent Mason several text messages, although she didn't expect him to be able to get back to her at this point. But of course, no news only led to more anxiety.

Three hours later, word came that the fire was under control. And when Nya saw fire trucks driving by the studio, she knew the firefighters were returning to their stations.

"They're heading back to the station," Sabrina said. "Let's go there. I have to know if Mason is okay."

Sabrina had already rescheduled her appointments for today, unable to concentrate on work until she knew if Mason was all right. "That's a great idea," Nya agreed. "Let's go."

When they arrived at Station Two, the ladder truck was just being backed into the bay. Nya hastily pulled the car up to the curb, and Sabrina was darting out even before it was fully parked. Nya did the same, running toward the first firefighter she saw.

"Tyler," she said breathlessly, her stomach lurching. "Is Tyler McKenzie okay?"

In the corner of her eye, she saw Sabrina throwing her arms around Mason. At six foot six, he was easy to pick out in a crowd. Nya was relieved, but the fact that Tyler wasn't with him made her worry even more.

"There's been a lot of chaos," the guy said. "I don't know. He may be at the hospital. I'm heading there now."

Nya flinched, the pain in her gut as intense as if someone had just hit her with a crowbar. Oh, God. Tyler was at the hospital? How badly had he been hurt?

"How hurt is he?" Nya asked, emotion clogging her voice. But the firefighter was already disappearing into the bay.

She stifled a sob…then thought that her eyes were playing tricks on her. Because she thought she saw Tyler jump down from the pump truck in the bay.

"Tyler?" she asked, confused.

He looked her way. It *was* him! Waves of relief washed over her.

"Tyler!" She ran toward him. "Oh, my God!" she sobbed. "I heard a firefighter was killed. I was so scared that it was you."

"I'm okay," Tyler said, sounding glum. "But four firefighters were injured, and yeah, one of our guys was killed. Dean Dunbar. He's got a wife, twin boys." He shook his head.

Nya's heart broke for him. "Oh, Tyler. I'm so sorry. That's devastating news." She wanted to wrap her arms around him, offer him support as he endured the pain of losing a friend. But she no longer had that right.

"We're all planning to head to the hospital, be there for the guys who were hurt." Tyler swallowed.

"I was so worried," Nya said softly. "I didn't know if you were hurt, or killed…"

"I was never really in any danger, since I operate the pump truck."

"Oh." She should have known that. But with the news that a firefighter had been killed, she'd been so beside herself that she hadn't been able to think clearly.

Looking up at him, she could see pain and frustration in his eyes, and knew it was the weight of the situation. A firefighter had died. Maybe this wasn't the time to talk to him about their relationship.

No. She wasn't going to walk away from him without letting him know how she felt.

She sucked in a breath filled with fear. Then she looked Tyler in the eyes.

"I thought I'd lost you forever. I thought I'd never get another chance to tell you that I love you and to make things right. I know this is a bad time, and a lot is going on. But there's never a right time, is there? And what happened today has driven home the point that life is short. So I want you to hear me out, Tyler. I want to make you understand. I get it now. Over the past week, I finally figured out what you've been trying to tell me all along. That I should be believing in myself. Not just when it comes to my career. But when it comes to me as a person." She paused, exhaled sharply. "I found everything I ever wanted with you, and I blew it because on some level I just didn't think I was worthy of your love. I didn't believe you'd want to stay with me forever. So many things have failed in my life. And I guess there was a part of me that just didn't believe good things would happen for me. It wasn't you, Tyler. It was me." A tear rolled down her cheek. "The ironic thing is that you're the one who's done the most to encourage me, to get me to believe in my dreams." Her voice cracked. "And I pushed away the one good thing to really come into my life in a long, long time."

"Nya…"

"No." She squared her shoulders, determined not to cry. She was here to fight for her man. "I own what I did, and I'm here to tell you that I'll *never* doubt you again. I love you, and I believe that you love me, too." She tried to read the expression in his eyes, but wasn't sure that she was getting through to him. "I want you back. And I'm not gonna leave your life without a fight. So you'd better get used to seeing me here every day for as long as it takes for you to believe me." She didn't flinch as she stared at him. She wanted him to know that she no longer had any doubts. "Tyler, I know we can be great together. Please, give us that chance."

Taking off his gloves, Tyler stepped toward her. Gently, he touched her cheek with his fingertips. Nya turned her face into his hand. Oh, how she had missed his touch.

"A lot has happened today," he said softly. "Losing Dean has reminded me and everyone here that life can change in an instant." He trailed his fingers along her jawbone then captured her chin between his thumb and forefinger. "You're right, Nya. We can be great together. I've known that for a long time. But I needed for you to know it, too. I was angry, yes. But it didn't take me long to realize that I didn't handle things the right way. If I'd been honest with you about Carol, you wouldn't have had to be insecure."

"No, Tyler. It was my fault."

"Shhh," he said. "The time for blame is over. The point

is, every day I've wanted to go to you, tell you that I want you in my life. But I didn't want to rush things. The important things in life are worth the wait. And I wanted to give you enough time to be certain about me, about *us*. I didn't want you running back to me just because you felt bad about what had happened and you wanted to make things right. I wanted to give you time to realize that you don't have to be afraid to let me love you."

A shiver of desire ran down her spine at his words. "Oh, Tyler. I'm not afraid. Not anymore."

He slipped an arm around her waist and pulled her against him. He smelled of soot, and his bunker gear was rough against her body, but she would take it. A million times she would take it.

"Good," he said. "Because I love you, baby. And I don't want to waste another moment without you. I'm yours…if you'll have me."

"If I'll have you?" Nya beamed and threw her arms around his neck. "You're never getting rid of me. Oh, Tyler. I love you. So much."

Tyler gave her a soft kiss. "Thank you."

Nya eyed him curiously. "For what?"

"For kissing me at the calendar fund-raiser. Because that's when I fell for you, that very first night when you kissed me."

Nya chuckled. "Really? You didn't think I was crazy?"

"A little crazy," he admitted. "But then you made me a little crazy. Crazy for you."

"Aww." Nya smiled. "You always say the right thing."

"I mean it, sweetheart. You're the one for me."

Warmth filled Nya's heart.

"Kiss me," Tyler whispered.

So she did.

And just like the first time, she felt sparks. Nya knew

that for as long as she lived, she would always feel sparks when she kissed this incredible man.

And finally, Nya had found her Mr. Right.

* * * * *

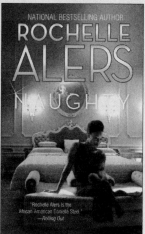

REQUEST YOUR FREE BOOKS!

2 FREE NOVELS
PLUS 2 FREE GIFTS!

KIMANI™
ROMANCE

Love's ultimate destination!

Will her vacation
fling turn into a
forever love?

All of Me

SHERYL LISTER

Declaring a "dating hiatus" was an easy decision for teacher
Karen Morris. She intends to unwind and enjoy a luxurious
Caribbean cruise solo, but businessman Damian Bradshaw
manages to change her mind. They ignite an insatiable need
that neither can deny… Will the promise of a bright future
be enough to rehabilitate their reluctant hearts?

Available January 2015 wherever books are sold!